The Camel closed up until it was flying beside him; the pilot smiling. Biggles showed his teeth in what he imagined to be an answering smile. 'You swine,' he breathed: 'you dirty, unutterable, murdering swine! I'm going to kill you if it's the last thing I do on earth.' Something made him glance upwards. Five Fokker tri-planes were coming down on him like bolts from the blue. 'So, that's it, is it?' he muttered. 'You're the bait and I'm the fish. That's your game. Well, they'll get me, but you're getting yours first.'

Captain W. E. Johns was born in Hertfordshire in 1893. He flew with the Royal Flying Corps in the First World War and made a daring escape from a German prison camp in 1918. Between the wars he edited *Flying* and *Popular Flying* and became a writer for the Ministry of Defence. The first Biggles story, *Biggles the Camels are Coming* was published in 1932, and W. E. Johns went on to write a staggering 102 Biggles titles before his death in 1968.

www.**randomhousechildrens**.co.uk

BIGGLES BOOKS
PUBLISHED IN THIS EDITION

BIGGLES
the CAMELS
ARE COMING

CAPTAIN W.E. JOHNS

RED FOX

Red Fox would like to express their grateful thanks
for help given in the preparation of these editions to Jennifer Schofield,
author of *By Jove, Biggles*, Linda Shaughnessy of A. P. Watt Ltd
and especially to the late John Trendler.

BIGGLES THE CAMELS ARE COMING
A RED FOX BOOK 9781782952114

First published in Great Britain by John Hamilton, London 1932
Published as *Biggles, Pioneer Air Fighter* by Armada 1982

This Red Fox edition published 2003

Red Fox Books are published by Random House Children's Publishers UK,
61–63 Uxbridge Road, London W5 5SA
A Random House Group Company

Addresses for companies within The Random House Group Limited
can be found at: www.randomhouse.co.uk/offices.htm

THE RANDOM HOUSE GROUP Limited Reg. No. 954009

A CIP catalogue record for this book is available from the British Library.

The Random House Group Limited supports The Forest Stewardship
Council® (FSC®), the leading international forest-certification organisation.
Our books carrying the FSC label are printed on FSC®-certified paper.
FSC is the only forest-certification scheme supported by the leading
environmental organisations, including Greenpeace. Our
paper procurement policy can be found at
www.randomhouse.co.uk/environment

MIX
Paper from
responsible sources
FSC® C016897

Printed and bound in Great Britain by Clays Ltd, St Ives plc

Contents

Foreword

Captain James Bigglesworth is a fictitious character, yet he could have been found in any R.F.C.* mess during those great days of 1917 and 1918 when air combat had become the order of the day and air duelling was a fine art. 'Biggles,' as I have said, did not exist under that name, yet he represents the spirit of the R.F.C.—daring and deadly when in the air, devil-may-care and debonair when on the ground.

To readers who are unfamiliar with the conditions that prevailed in the blue skies of France during the last two years of the War, it may seem unlikely that so many adventures could have fallen to the lot of one man. In those eventful years, every day—and I might almost say every hour—brought adventure, tragic or humorous, to the man in the air, and as we sat in our cockpits warming up our engines for the dawn 'show**', no one could say what the end of the day would bring, or whether he would be alive to see it.

Again, it may seem improbable that any one man could have been involved in so many hazardous undertakings, and yet survive. That may be true; sooner or later most War pilots met the inevitable fate of the flying fighter. I sometimes wonder how any of us sur-

* Royal Flying Corps 1914–1918. An army corps responsible for military aeronautics, renamed the Royal Air Force (RAF) when amalgamated with the Royal Naval Air Service on 1st April 1918.
** Slang: operational flight into enemy-held territory.

7

vived, yet there were some who seemed to bear a charmed life. William Bishop, the British ace, René Fonck, the French ace and prince of air duellists, and, on the other side, Ernst Udet, and many others, fought hundreds of battles in the air and survived thousands of hours of deadly peril. Every day incredible deeds of heroism were performed by pilots whose names are unknown, and had the Victoria Cross been awarded consistently, hundreds instead of a few would have worn the coveted decoration.

Nowhere are the curious whims of Lady Luck so apparent as in the air. Lothar von Richthofen, brother of the famous ace, shot down forty British machines; he was killed in a simple cross-country flight shortly after the War. Nungesser, the French champion of forty-five air battles, was drowned, and McKeever, Canadian ace of thirty victories, was killed in a skidding motor-car. Captain 'Jock' McKay of my Squadron survived three years air warfare, only to be killed by 'archie*' an hour before the Armistice was signed. Lieutenant A. E. Amey, who fought his first and last fight beside me, had not even unpacked his kit! I have spun into the ground out of control from 6,000 feet, yet I am alive to tell the tale. Gordon, of my Squadron, made a good landing, but bumped on an old road that ran across the aerodrome, turned turtle, and broke his neck.

Again, should the sceptic think I have been guilty of exaggeration, I would say that exaggeration is almost impossible where air combat is concerned. The terrific speed at which a dog-fight took place and the amazing manner in which machines appeared from nowhere, and could disappear, apparently into thin air, was so

* Slang: Anti-aircraft gunfire

bewildering as to baffle description. It is beyond my ability to convey adequately the sensation of being one of ten or a dozen machines, zooming, whirling, and diving among the maze of pencil lines that marked the track of tracer bullets.* One could not exaggerate the stunning horror of seeing two machines collide head-on a few yards away, and words have yet to be coined to express that tightening of the heart-strings that comes of seeing one of your own side roaring down in a sheet of flame. Seldom was any attempt made by spectators to describe these things at the time; they were best forgotten.

It is not surprising that many strange incidents occurred, incidents which were never written down on combat reports, but were whispered 'with wrinkled brows, with nods, and rolling eyes' in dim corners of the hangars while we were waiting for the order to start up or for the 'late birds' to come home to roost. It was 'H', a tall South African S.E.** pilot who came in white-faced and told me that he had just shot down a Camel*** by mistake. It was the Camel pilot's fault. He playfully zoomed over the S.E., apparently out of sheer light-heartedness. 'H' told me that he started shooting when he only saw the shadow; he turned and saw the red, white, and blue circles, but it was too late. He had already gripped the Bowden control† and fired a burst of not more than five rounds. He had fired

* Phosphorus-loaded bullets whose course through the air could be seen by day and by night.
** Scouting experimental single-seater British biplane fighter in service 1917–1920
*** Sopwith Camel, a single-seater biplane fighter with twin machine guns synchronised to fire through the propeller. See front cover for illustration.
† The 'trigger' to fire the guns, usually fitted to a pilot's control column.

9

hundreds of rounds at enemy aircraft without hitting one, but the Camel fell in flames. He asked me if he should report it, and I, rightly or wrongly, said no, for nothing could bring the Camel back. 'H' went West* soon afterwards.

What of 'T—L—' still in the Service, who was attacked by a Belgian scout? For ten minutes he endeavoured to escape, and then, exasperated, he turned and shot the Belgian down, narrowly escaping court-martial as a consequence. Almost everybody has heard the story told by Boelcke, the German ace — and he was a man to be believed — of how he once found a British machine with a dead crew flying a ghostly course amid the clouds. On another occasion he shot down an F.E.** which, spinning viciously, threw its observer out behind the German lines and the pilot behind the British lines. What of the R.E.8*** that landed perfectly behind our lines with pilot and observer stiff and stark in their cockpits! The R.E.8 was not an easy machine to land at any time, as those who flew it will bear witness.

René Fonck once shot down a German machine which threw out its pilot; machine and man fell straight through the middle of a formation of Spads below without touching one of them! The German pilot was Wissemann, who had just shot down Guynemer, Fonck's friend and brother ace, but he did not know that at the time. The coincidence is worth noting. Madon, another ace, once attacked a German two-seater at point-blank

* Slang: was killed
** British two-seater pusher biplane with the engine behind the pilot and the gunner in the forward cockpit.
*** British two-seater biplane designed for reconnaissance and artillery purposes.

range—his usual method. A bullet struck the goggles off the Boche* observer and sent them whirling into the air; Madon caught them on his wires and brought them home. When Warneford shot down his Zeppelin** one of the crew jumped from the blazing airship, and after falling a distance generally believed to be about 200 feet, crashed through the roof of a convent and landed on a bed which had just been vacated by a nun. He lived to tell the tale. When it comes to pure coincidence the following tale goes rather farther than a fiction writer would dare to venture. It was told to me by the principal actors themselves shortly after they had been led into the prison camp where I was confined. They themselves were still finding the thing difficult to believe.

It came about through Pat Manley losing his propeller. For the benefit of the reader who is not conversant with air jargon, to lose one's propellor does not mean that it fell off, or anything like that. It is said to be 'lost' when it stops turning round.

Pat Manley and Swayze were friends who joined the infantry and came over with the Canadian contingent. They were hit on the same day, went to different hospitals and completely lost touch with each other. A year later Pat, beetling around over the line in a Bristol Fighter***, saw another Bristol going down under a cloud of enemy aircraft. He throttled back and put his nose down in a steep dive to join the party; but he was too late and he saw the other Bristol crash in a field.

* Derogatory term for the Germans
** Airships of rigid construction used by the Germans mainly over Britain for strategic bombing and reconnaissance
*** British two-seater fighter with remarkable manoeuvrability, in service 1917 onwards. It had one fixed Vickers gun for the pilot and one or two mobile Lewis guns for the observer/gunner.

Perceiving that no good purpose could be served by hanging around, Pat was about to make for a healthier quarter of the sky, when, as previously stated, he lost his propeller. Being very low he was unable to dive to get it back so he landed beside the crash, just in time to see Swayze crawl out. Thus, they were both taken prisoner within one minute of each other on the same field in France.

Here is another story which illustrates the sort of thing that could happen to a pilot in those days. It happened I believe to Carter, who told me the story when we were prisoners of war together. I see he is now commanding the Iraqian Air Force. He was a Camel pilot then, and was so tickled to death one day at finding a column of enemy troops on the march that he could not tear himself away from them.

He amused himself for a time by unloading his 20-lb. Cooper bombs on them, and when this began to pall he came lower and sprayed them with his gun. So fascinating did this pastime become, and so vastly entertaining were the antics of the warriors below in their frantic haste to remove themselves from the locality, that he quite failed to notice the telegraph wires which, as so often happens, accompanied the road on its winding way. He hit the wires at the bottom of a zoom and took them, together with a snapped-off post or two, for a short joy-ride. It was a pity he could not have given the troops a treat by taking them all the way home, but the Camel, not being designed for such work, gave up the ghost and spread itself over the landscape.

The tables now being somewhat turned, his erstwhile victims proceeded to amuse themselves by battering him to pulp with their rifle butts, a comparatively tame pursuit from which they were only compelled to desist by the arrival of a senior officer.

Carter was taken to the same hospital as the men he had wounded, where a state of affairs prevailed for the next week or so that can be better imagined than described!

One could go on with such stories indefinitely, but these should be sufficient to show that, in the air at least, truth is stranger than fiction.

Many of the adventures that are ascribed to Biggles did actually occur, and are true in their essential facts. Students of air history will have no difficulty in identifying them. In many cases the officers themselves are still alive and serving in the Royal Air Force.

Finally, I hope that from a perusal of these pages a younger generation of air fighters may learn something of the tricks of the trade, of the traps and pitfalls that beset the unwary, for I fear that many of the lessons which we learned in the hard school of war are being rapidly obscured by the mists of peace-time theory. In air-fighting, one week of war experience is worth a year of peace-time practice. In peace a man may make a mistake—and live. He may not even know of his mistake. If he makes that same mistake in war—he dies, unless it is his lucky day, in which case the error is so vividly brought to his notice that he is never guilty of it again.

No one can say just how he will react when, for the first time, he hears the flack! flack! flack! of bullets ripping through his machine. The sound has turned boys into grey-faced men, and even hardened campaigners who learnt their business on the ground have felt their lips turn dry.

In the following pages certain expressions occur from

time to time in connection with the tactics of air combat which may seem to the layman to be out of proportion to their importance. For instance, he will read of 'getting into the sun.' It is quite impossible for anybody who does not fly to realize what this means and how utterly impossible it is to see what is going on in that direction, particularly when the sun is low and one is flying west. To fly into the face of the setting sun can be uncomfortable at any time, but the strain of trying to peer into the glare, knowing that it may discharge a squadron of death-spitting devils at any moment, becomes positive torture after a time; at least, I found it so.

It should also be remembered that an aeroplane is an extremely small vehicle and difficult to see. When one is on the ground it is the noise of the engine that almost invariably first attracts attention, and but for the unmistakable tell-tale hum few would be seen at all. In the air, the roar of one's own engine drowns all other sound, and one is therefore dependent upon sight alone for detecting the presence of other aircraft. This fact should constantly be borne in mind when reading stories of the air, and particularly of air combat.

Constant reference is also made to 'archie.' Most people know by now that this was not an old friend whom we called by his Christian name. There was nothing friendly about archie. On the contrary, he often bit you when you were least expecting it, but on the whole his bark was worse than his bite. Archie was the war-pilot's nick-name for anti-aircraft gun-fire. During the War archie batteries stretched from the North Sea to the Swiss Frontier;* his appearance in the sky was accepted as a matter of course, and dodging him was

* i.e. along the front line trenches where the opposing armies faced one another.

part of the daily round. After a time one became accustomed to it and ignored it unless it was very bad.

Lingfield, 1932.   W. E. J.

The word 'Hun' as used in this book, was the common generic term for anything belonging to the enemy. It was used in a familiar sense, rather than derogatory. Witness the fact that in the R.F.C. a hun was also a pupil at flying training school.

W. E. J.

Chapter 1
The White Fokker

To the casual observer, the attitude of the little group of pilots clustered around the entrance of B Flight hangar was one of complete nonchalance. MacLaren, still wearing the tartans and glengarry of his regiment,* a captain's stars on his sleeve, squatted uncomfortably on an upturned chock. To a student of detail the steady spiral of smoke from the quickly-drawn cigarette, lighted before the last half was consumed, gave the lie to his bored expression. Quinan, his 'maternity'** tunic flapping open at the throat, hands thrust deep into the pockets of his slacks, leaning carelessly against the flimsy structure of the temporary hangar, gnawed the end of a dead match with slow deliberation. Swayne, bareheaded, the left shoulder of his tunic as black as ink with burnt castor oil, seated on an empty oil drum, was nervously plucking little tufts of wool from the tops of his sheepskin boots. Bigglesworth, popularly known as Biggles, a slight, fair-haired, good-looking lad still in his teens, but an acting Flight-Commander, was talking, not of wine or women as novelists would have us believe, but of a new fusee spring for a Vickers***

---

* Officers transferring from the army to the air corps were allowed to retain their previous regiment's uniform.
** Tunic with a flap across the front which fastened at the side, not in the middle.
*** Machine gun firing a continuous stream of bullets at one squeeze of the trigger.

gun which would speed it up another hundred rounds a minute.

His deep-set hazel eyes were never still and held a glint of yellow fire that somehow seemed out of place in a pale face upon which the strain of war, and sight of sudden death, had already graven little lines. His hands, small and delicate as a girl's, fidgeted continually with the tunic fastening at his throat. He had killed a man not six hours before. He had killed six men during the past month—or was it a year?—he had forgotten. Time had become curiously telescoped lately. What did it matter, anyway? He knew he had to die some time and had long ago ceased to worry about it. His careless attitude suggested complete indifference, but the irritating little falsetto laugh which continually punctuated his tale betrayed the frayed condition of his nerves.

From the dim depths of the hangar half a dozen tousled-headed ack-emmas* watched their officers furtively as they pretended to work on a war-scarred Camel. One habit all ranks had in common: every few seconds their eyes would study the western horizon long and anxiously. A visiting pilot would have known at once that the evening patrol was overdue. As a matter of fact, it should have been in ten minutes before.

'Here they come!' The words were sufficient to cause all further pretence to be abandoned; officers and men together were on their feet peering with hand-shaded eyes towards the setting sun whence came the rhythmic purr of rotary engines, still far away. Three specks became visible against the purple glow; a scarcely

* Slang: Air Mechanics.

audible sigh was the only indication of the nervous tension that the appearance of the three machines had broken. The door of the Squadron office opened and Major Mullen, the C.O.,* came out. He would not have admitted that he too had shared the common anxiety, but he fell in line with the watchers on the tarmac to await the arrival of the overdue machines.

The three Camels were barely half a mile away, at not more than a 1,000 feet, when a new note became audible above the steady roar of the engines. It was the shrill scream of wind-torn wings and wires. Whoof! Whoof! Whoof! Three white puffs** of smoke appeared high above the now gliding Camels. Bang!—Whoof! Bang!—Whoof!—the archie battery at the far end of the aerodrome took up the story. Not a man of the waiting group moved, but every eye shifted to a gleaming speck which had detached itself from the dark-blue vault above. A white-painted Fokker D.VII*** was coming down like a meteor behind the rearmost Camel. There was a glittering streak of tracer. The Camel staggered for a moment and then plunged straight to earth. At the rattle of guns the other two Camels opened their engines and half-rolled convulsively. The leader, first out, was round like a streak at the Fokker, which, pulling out of its dive, had shot up to 3,000 feet in one tremendous zoom, turned, and was streaking for the line. The stricken Camel hit the ground just inside the aerodrome; a sheet of flame leapt skywards.

From first to last the whole incident had occupied

* Commanding Officer.
** In general, British anti-aircraft fire gave off white smoke and German anti-aircraft fire gave off black smoke.
*** Very efficient German single-seater biplane fighter with two forward firing guns.

perhaps three seconds, during which time none of the spell-bound spectators on the tarmac had either moved or spoken. The C.O. recovered himself first, and with a bitter curse raced towards the Lewis gun* mounted outside his office. Half-way he changed his mind and swung round towards the blazing Camel in the wake of the flying ambulance only to stop dead, throw up his hands with a despairing gesture, and turn again towards the hangar.

'Get out, you fool; where the hell do you think you are going—he's home by now,' he snapped at Bigglesworth, who was feverishly clambering, cap and goggles-less, into a Camel.

As the two surviving Camels taxied in, a babble of voices broke loose. Mahoney, who had led the flight, leaned swaying for a moment against the fuselage of his machine. His lips moved, but no sound came; he seemed to be making a tremendous effort to pull himself together. His eyes roved round the aerodrome to identify the pilot of the other Camel. Manley, half-falling out of the cockpit of the other machine, hurried towards him. 'All right, old lad, take it easy, it wasn't your fault,' he said quickly. Mahoney's lips continued to move as he struggled to speak. 'It was Norman—poor little devil! First time over, too—the damn swine—he didn't give him a chance—not a b—' His voice rose to shrill crescendo.

'Stop that!' cut in the C.O. quickly, and then more quietly, 'Steady, Mahoney.' For a moment the Flight-Commander and his Commanding Officer eyed each other grimly. Mahoney's eyes fell first. Slowly he took

---

* Light machine gun, used both on the ground and also often by the observer/gunner in two-seater aircraft.

off his sidcot* and threw it on the ground with studied deliberation. Cap and goggles followed, leaving that part of his face which they had protected like a white mask.

'Officers in the Orderly Room,** please,' said the C.O., turning on his heel. Mahoney lit a cigarette and followed the little group moving towards the Squadron office.

'Sit down, everybody,' began Major Mullen. 'A bad show. I blame no one. Anybody could have been caught the same way. It might have been me, or it might have been you, Mahoney. From some points of view it was a low-down trick; from others, well, it was a smart piece of work; anyway, the fellow was within his rights. He's done it before, farther north; I've heard about it. He did it three times at 197 Squadron, once as they were taking off. He'll try it again, and if he pulls it off again here it's our own funeral. We've had our lesson. We'll get him; we've *got* to get him. You know the unwritten law about having an officer shot down on his own aerodrome? We can't show our faces in another mess until we *do* get him. You know what Wing*** will say about this. That's all. Go and get a drink, Mahoney. I'll see Flight-Commanders here in half an hour.'

An hour later Major Mullen was running over the result of the conference. 'I think Mahoney's right,' he said. 'The Fokker probably came over the line at eighteen or twenty thousand with his engine off. He must

---

* A thick, padded garment worn by aircrew.
** A room or office used for day to day Squadron business.
*** The administrative headquarters. Each Wing commanded several squadrons. It was headed by a Lieutenant-Colonel.

have been watching you all the time, Mahoney. He knew that you were at the end of the patrol and hadn't enough juice left to go back after him. All right, then. Mahoney, you'll take the patrol in the morning; come back in the ordinary way when it's over. Bigglesworth, you'll take your Flight to the ceiling*. Hang around over Mossyface Wood until you see Mahoney coming back and then follow him home. Stay as high as you can and don't take your eyes off Mahoney's Flight for a moment. If the Fokker comes down, one of you should get him. If he doesn't show up, we'll keep it up until he does. It means long hours, but we can't help that. All clear? Good. Let's go and eat.'

The following morning Mahoney was bringing his Flight back by way of Mossyface Wood as arranged. His altimeter registered 10,000 feet, Often he leaned back in his cockpit and studied the sky above him long and earnestly for a sign of Bigglesworth's Flight, but a film of cirrus cloud far above concealed everything beyond it. Against that cloud a machine would show up like a fly on a white ceiling; his roving eyes searched it, section by section, from horizon to horizon, but not a speck broke its pristine surface. At 6.30 he turned his nose for home according to plan, maintaining his height until he reached the line and only taking his eyes from aloft to see that Manley and Forrest in the other two Camels were in place. He crossed the line in the inevitable flurry of archie, and started a long glide towards the aerodrome. A cluster of black archie bursts far away to the north showed where some allied machines were moving; there was apparently nothing else in the

* Slang: as high as their power will allow.

21

sky, yet he felt uneasy. What was the other side of that cloud? He wished he could see. Every fibre of his war-tried airman's instinct reacted against that opaque curtain. He flew with his eyes ever turned upwards. Suddenly he caught his breath. For a fraction of a second a black spot had appeared against the cloud and disappeared again almost before he could fasten his eyes on it. Keeping his eyes on the spot he raised his left arm, shook his wings, opened up his engine, and warmed his guns with a short burst. What was going on up there? He was soon to know. A machine, whether friend or foe he could not tell, wrapped in a sheet of flame, hurtled downwards through the cloud into oblivion, leaving a long plume of black smoke in its wake. Mahoney stiffened in his seat. Next came a Camel spinning wildly out of control. Then another Camel, streaking for home, followed by five Fokkers. Mahoney muttered a curse through his clenched teeth and swung round and up in a wide arc, knowing as he did so that he could never get up to the Fokkers in time to help the Camel, now crossing the line at a speed which threatened to take its wings off. A barrage of archie appeared between the Fokkers and the Camel, and the black-crossed machines, after a moment's hesitation, turned and dived for home. Mahoney raced after the solitary Camel, whose pilot, seeing him coming, throttled back to wait for him.

They landed together and the C.O. ran out to meet them. Bigglesworth, the pilot of the lone Camel, was out first. 'I've lost Swayne and Maddison,' he said grimly, as the others joined him. 'I've lost Swayne and Maddison,' he repeated. 'I've lost Swayne and Maddison, can't you hear me?' he said yet again. 'What the hell are you looking at me like that for?'

'Nobody's looking at you, Biggles,' broke in the C.O. 'Take it steady and tell us what happened.'

Biggles groped for his cigarette case. 'We're boobs,' he muttered bitterly. 'Pilots, eh? We ought to be riding scooters in Kensington Gardens. What did we do? We did just what they damn well knew we'd do, and they were waiting for us, the whole bunch of 'em!' He passed his hand over his face wearily as his passion spent itself. He tossed his flying-coat on to the tarmac and went on quietly. 'I was up 20,000, or as near as I could get, waiting. So were they, but I didn't see 'em at first; must have been hiding in that damn soup. I saw Mahoney coming, heading for Mossy-face, and then I saw the White Fokker, by himself. He wasn't there for you, Mahoney, he was there to get me down. I didn't look up and that's a fact. I saw the Fokker going down and I fell for it. I thought he was cold meat and I went down after him. Where the others came from I don't know. They were into us just before we hit the cloud. The first thing I saw was the tracer, and poor Mad going down in flames next to me. I went after the white bird like a sack of bricks, but I lost him in the cloud. Swayne had gone, so I made for home, and I'm damn lucky to get here. That's all.'

He turned and strode off towards the mess. Major Mullen watched him go without a word.

'I'll have a word with you, Mahoney, and you, Mac,' he said, and together they entered the orderly room. 'We've got to do something about this,' he began briskly. 'We shall all be for Home Establishment* if it goes on. Bigglesworth's going to bits fast, but if he can get that Fokker it will restore his confidence. We've

---

* Posted home to the UK for a non-combat role.

23

lost three machines in two days and we are going to lose more if we don't stop that white devil.'

Bigglesworth entered. 'Hullo, Biggles, sit down,' said the C.O. quietly. Biggles nodded.

'I've been trying to work this out, sir,' he began, 'and this is my idea. First of all you'll notice that this Fokker doesn't go for the leaders. He always picks on one of the rear men in the formation; you saw how he got Norman. All right. Tomorrow we'll do the usual patrol of three. Mahoney or Mac can lead and I'll be in the formation. I'll pretend I'm scared of everything and sideslip away from every archie burst. Coming home I'll hang back and the others will go on ahead without me. That should bring him down. If he comes I'll be ready and we'll see who can shoot straightest and quickest. If he gets me—well—he gets me, but if he doesn't, I'll get him. He'll have height of me I know, and that's where he holds the cards. I've got an idea about that, too. Someone will have to take every available machine and wait upstairs to keep the others off if they try to butt in. Don't make a move unless they start coming down; let them make the first move, that should give you height of 'em. I'm having an extra tank put in my machine so that I'll have some spare juice when he'll reckon I've none left, in case I want to turn back.'

The C.O. nodded: 'That sounds all right to me,' he said. 'I've only one thing to say, and that is, I'll take the party up topsides. You can rely on me to keep anybody busy who starts to interfere with your show. Good enough! We'll try it in the morning.'

The pink hue of dawn had turned to turquoise when Mahoney turned for home at the end of the dawn patrol. One machine of his Flight was lagging back, and for the hundredth time he turned and waved for it to close up, smiling as he did so. Biggles had played the novice to perfection. Even now, a bracket of archie* sent him careering wide from the formation. Mahoney's roving eyes were never still; slowly and methodically they searched every section of air around, above, and below. Far above them a Rumpler** was making for home followed by a long line of white archie, but he made no attempt to pursue it. Far to the north-east a formation of 'Nines' was heading out into the blue; high above them he could just make out the escorting Bristols. He gazed upwards long and anxiously. He could see nothing, but he knew that somewhere in the blue void at least one formation of fighters was watching him that very moment. Biggles too was watching; he had pushed his goggles up to see better. Now and then he dived a little to gain speed so that the watchers above might think he was trying to keep in position. They were going home now; if the White Fokker was about today he would soon have to show up. The formation started to lose height slowly; Biggles warmed his gun every few minutes, but still kept up the pretence of bad flying.

They were well over the line now. The two other Camels had dropped to 5,000 feet, but he hung back slightly above them. Once he threw a loop to show his apparent relief at being safely back over his own side of the line. Dash it, why didn't the fellow come? The two other Camels were nearly a mile ahead when Biggles suddenly focussed his eyes upon a spot far above and held it. Was it, or was it not? Yes! Far above

* A bracket is when shells burst on either side of a target.
** German two-seater biplane for observation and light bombing raids.

25

and behind him a tiny light flashed for an instant, and he knew it for the sun striking the planes* of a machine, whether friend or foe he could not tell. He kept his eyes glued to the spot. He could see the machine now, a tiny black speck rapidly growing larger. Biggles smiled grimly. 'Here comes the hawk, I'm the sparrow. Well, we'll see.' The machine was plainly visible now, a Fokker D.VII. There was no sign of archie, so he concluded that the Fokker had shut his engine off and had not yet been seen from the ground. Biggles opened his throttle wide and put his nose down slightly in order to get as much speed as possible without alarming the enemy above. The Fokker was coming down now with the speed of light; a cluster of archie far above it showed that the pilot had cast concealment to the winds. Biggles pushed his nose down and raced for home. Speed—speed—speed—that was all he wanted now to take him up behind the Fokker. How near dare he let him come? Could the Fokker hit him first burst? He had to chance it. At 200 feet a stream of tracer spurted from the Fokker's Spandaus.** Biggles moved the rudder-bar, and, as the bullets streamed between his planes pulled the stick back into his stomach. Half-rolling off the top of the loop and looking swiftly for his adversary, he caught his breath as the Fokker swept by a bare ten feet away. He had a vivid impression of the face of the man in the pilot's seat, looking at him. Biggles was on its tail in a flash. Through his sights he saw it still climbing. Rat-tat-tat—he cursed luridly as he hammered at the gun which had jammed at the

* The wings of an aircraft were also called its planes.
** German machine guns were often referred to as Spandaus, due to the fact that many were manufactured at Spandau, Germany.

critical moment. The Fokker had Immelmanned* and was coming back at him now, but Biggles was ready, and pulled his nose up to take it head-on. Vaguely, out of the corner of his eye he saw another Fokker whirling down in a cloud of smoke and other planes above. The White Fokker swerved and he followed it round.

They were circling now, each machine in a vertical bank not a hundred feet apart, the Fokker slowly gaining height. Biggles thought swiftly, 'Ten more circles and he's above me and then it's goodbye.' There was one chance left, a desperate one. He knew that the second he pulled out of the circle the Fokker would be on his tail and get a shot at him. Whatever he did the Fokker would still be on his tail at the finish. If he rolled, the Fokker would roll too, and still be in the same position. If he spun, the Fokker would spin; there was no shaking off a man who knew his job, but if he shot out of the circle he might get a lead of three hundred feet, and if he could loop fast enough he might get the Fokker from the top of his loop as it passed underneath in his wake. If he was too quick they would collide; no matter, they would go to Kingdom Come together. A feeling of fierce exultation swept over him. 'Come on, you devil!' he cried, 'I'll take your lead,' and shot out of the circle. He shoved his stick forward savagely as something smashed through the root of the nearest centre-section strut,** and then he pulled it back in a swift zoom. A fleeting glance over his shoulder showed the Fokker three hundred feet behind. He

* This manoeuvre consists of a half roll off the top of a loop thereby quickly reversing the direction of flight. It was named after Max Immelmann, successful German fighter pilot 1914–1916 with seventeen victories who was the first to use this turn in combat.
** Rigid supports between the wings and fuselage of a biplane or triplane.

pulled the stick right back into his stomach in a flick loop and his eyes sought the sights as he pressed his triggers. Blue sky—blue sky—the horizon—green fields—where was the Fokker? Ah! There he was, flying straight into his stream of tracer. He saw the pilot slump forward in his seat. He held the loop a moment longer and then flung the Camel over on to an even keel, looking swiftly for the Fokker as he did so. It was rocketting like a hard-hit pheasant. It stalled; its nose whipped over and with the engine racing it roared down in an almost vertical dive. Biggles saw the top plane fold back, and then he looked away feeling suddenly limp and very tired.

A mile away five straight-winged machines were making for the line, followed by four Camels; another Camel was trying to land in a ploughed field below. Even as he watched it the wheels touched and it somersaulted; a figure scrambled out and looked upwards, waving. Biggles side-slipped down into the next field and landed. Major Mullen, the pilot of the wrecked Camel, ran to meet him.

'Good boy,' he cried, 'you brought it off.'

Chapter 2
The Packet

'Two no-trumps.' Biggles, newly appointed to Captain's rank since his affair with the White Fokker, made the bid as if he held all the court cards in the pack.

'Two diamonds,' offered Quinan, sitting on his left.

Mahoney, Biggle's partner, looked across the table apologetically. 'No bid,' he said, wearily.

'Hell's bells, don't you ever support your partner?' complained Biggles. 'You've sat there all the afternoon croaking "No bid" like a damned parrot. You ought to have a gramophone record made of it, and keep it with your scoring block.'

'Who the devil are you grousing at?' fired up Mahoney. 'Any fool could sit and chirp no-trumps if they held the paper you do. If you could only play the cards you hold we'd get a rubber sometimes, instead of being a thousand points down.'

'What sort of a game do you call this, anyway?' broke in Batson, the fourth player. 'Why don't you show each other your cards and have done with it?'

Major Mullen entered the ante-room. 'I want you, Biggles, when you've played the hand. Stand by, everybody; it's clearing,' he continued, addressing the othes in the room and referring to the steady drizzle which had washed out flying so far that day.

Biggles looked at the hand which his partner had laid on the table with disgust. The knave to two diamonds was his best suit. 'Clearing, eh?' he said, grimly.

'So am I. Holy smoke, what a mitt.' He was two down on the bid. He rose. 'Tot it up,' he invited his opponents, 'I'll settle when I come back.'

'No you don't, you settle now,' snapped Batson. 'Miller went West owing me seventy francs—you cough it up, Biggles.' Biggles reluctantly counted out some notes. 'Take it and I'll starve,' he grumbled. 'We'll finish this last rubber when I come back.' He followed Major Mullen to the Squadron office, where he found an officer awaiting them, whose red tabs showed that he came from a higher command.

'Captain Bigglesworth—Colonel Raymond,' began the C.O. 'This is the officer I was telling you about, sir.'

Biggles saluted and eyed the stranger curiously. The Colonel looked at him so long and earnestly that Biggles ran his mind swiftly over the events of the last few days, trying to recall some incident which might account for the senior officer's presence. 'Sit down, Bigglesworth,' said the Colonel at last, 'smoke if you like.' Biggles sat and lit a cigarette.

'You are wondering why I've sent for you,' began the Colonel. 'I'll tell you. Frankly, I'm going to ask you to undertake a tough proposition.' Biggles stiffened in his chair.

'First of all,' went on the Colonel, 'what I am going to tell you is secret. Not a word to anybody, and I mean that. Not one word. Now, this is the position. You know, of course, that we have—er—agents—operatives—call 'em what you like—over the line. They are usually taken over by aircraft; sometimes they drop by parachute and sometimes we land them, according to circumstances. Sometimes they come back; more often they do not. Sometimes the pilot who takes them over picks them up at a pre-arranged spot at a subsequent date. Sometimes—but never mind—that doesn't concern you.

'A fortnight ago such an agent went over. He did not come back. We know, never mind how, that he obtained what he went to fetch, which was, to be quite frank, a packet of plans. An officer went to fetch him by arrangement, but the enemy had evidently watched our man and wired* the field. When the F.E. pilot—it was at night—got to the field it was a death trap. The officer was killed landing. The operative bolted, but was taken. We have since received information that he has been shot. Before he was taken he managed to conceal the plans, and we know where they are. We want those plans badly—urgently; in three days they will be useless.'

'I see,' said Biggles slowly, 'and you want me to go and fetch them?'

'If you will.'

'May I ask roughly where they are?' said Biggles.

'You may,' replied the Colonel; 'they are near Ariet.'

'Ariet?' cried Biggles. 'Why 297 and 287 Squadrons are both nearer than we are; why not send them?'

'For two reasons,' replied Colonel Raymond, '297 Squadron is equipped with D.H.9's** and a "nine" could not get down in the field. Obviously, if it were possible, we should send an F.E. over at night, but, unfortunately, a night landing is out of the question. Only a single-seater could hope to get in, and then only by clever flying. A single-seater might just get into the

---

* strung wires across the field at head height so that any aeroplane attempting to land will run into them and crash.
** De Havilland 9—a two-seater British bomber with one fixed forward-firing gun for the pilot plus a mobile gun for the rear gunner/observer.

field, collect the plans, and get off again before the enemy arrived. We photographed the place at once, naturally. Here they are—take a look at them.' He tossed a packet of photographs casually to Biggles. 'The place is about two miles from where the disaster occurred, and the poor devil must have been taken somewhere near that spot.'

One glance showed Biggles that the Colonel had not underestimated the difficulty. 'From what height was this taken?' he asked, holding up a photograph on which was marked a small white cross.

'Six thousand feet,' replied the Colonel. 'The white mark is the position of the packet. When our man knew the game was up he shoved the plans down a rabbit-hole at the foot of a tree in the corner of that field. His last act was to release a pigeon, pin-pointing the position. The bird could not, of course, carry the plans.'

'Stout effort,' said Biggles approvingly. 'So the plans are in the corner of the field I land in. From this photo I should say that the field is about 150 yards long by 50 yards wide. I might just get in, but the wind would have to be right.'

'It is right, *now*,' replied the Colonel, softly but pointedly.

'Now?'

'Now!'

'What about 287 Squadron?' asked Biggles curiously. 'Don't think I am inquisitive, sir, but they've got S.E.5's and they are nearer than we are.'

'If you must know,' returned the Colonel, 'we have already been to them. They have lost two officers in the attempt and we can't ask them for another. Neither of them reached the field; archie got one, and we can only suppose that enemy aircraft got the other. You will pass both crashes on the way.'

'Thanks,' said Biggles grimly. 'I can find my way without them. It's about twenty miles over, isn't it?'

'About that, yes.'

'All right, sir,' said Biggles, 'I'll go, but I'd like to ask one thing.' He turned to Major Mullen. 'Do you mind if I ask for MacLaren or Mahoney to watch me from "upstairs"? If they could meet me on the way home it might help. I shall be low coming home—cold meat for any stray Hun that happens to be about?' He turned to Colonel Raymond. 'What would happen if I had to land with those plans on me?' he asked.

'I expect the enemy would shoot you,*' returned the Colonel. 'In fact, I am sure they would.'

'All right, sir,' said Biggles, 'as long as we understand. If my engine cuts out while I am over the other side those plans are going overboard before I hit the deck. I don't mind dying, but when I die, I'll die sitting down, like an officer and a gentleman—not standing with my back to a brick wall. If I come back, I shall have the plans with me—if they are still there.'

'That's fair enough,' agreed Colonel Raymond.

'May I take Mac and Mahoney with me to look after the ceiling?' he asked the C.O.

'Any objection, sir?' asked Major Mullen.

'None, as far as I am concerned,' replied the Colonel.

'Good; then I'll be off,' said Biggles, rising. 'Going to wait for the plans, sir? I shall be back within the hour, or not at all.'

'I'll wait,' said the Colonel gravely.

* Members of the forces captured during the War were entitled to be held prisoner and honourably treated but anyone engaged in spying (which included transporting a spy) was shot by firing squad.

Major Mullen accompanied Biggles to the door. 'Get those plans, Biggles,' he said, 'and the Squadron's name is on the top line. Fail—and it's mud. Good-bye and good luck.' A swift handshake and Biggles was on his way to the sheds.

As he gave instructions for his Camel to be started up, he noticed that the sun was already sinking in the west; he could not expect more than an hour and a half of daylight. He turned towards the Mess*, a burst of song greeting him as he opened the door.

'Mac! Mahoney! here a minute,' he called.

'What's the matter now, you hot-air merchant?' growled Mahoney as they advanced to meet him. 'Can't you—' Biggles cut him short.

'Show on,' he said crisply. 'I'm going to Ariet—to fetch a packet.'

'To Ariet?' said Mahoney incredulously.

'You'll get a packet all right,' sneered MacLaren, 'but why go to Ariet for it?'

'Never mind, I can't tell you,' said Biggles. 'Seriously, chaps, I'm going to land at Ariet. I shall go over high up, but I shall be damned low coming home, right on the carpet most of the way in all probability. Shan't have time to get any height. I'm going straight there and, I hope, straight back. You can help if you will by watching things up topsides. I've got to bring something back besides myself or I wouldn't ask you, and that's a fact. It's a long way over—twenty miles, and I expect every Hun in the sky will be looking for me as I come back. If they spot you they may not see me. That's all,' he concluded.

* The place where the officers eat and relax together.

34

'What the bl—' cut in Mahoney. Biggles cut him short.

'I'm off now,' he announced, 'may I expect to see you shortly?'

'Of course,' said Mahoney, 'I don't understand what it's all about and it seems a damn-fool business to me.' He glanced up and saw Colonel Raymond and Major Mullen walking towards the Mess. 'Blast these brass-hats*,' he growled. 'Why can't they stay at home on a dud day? Righto, laddie; see you presently.'

Twenty minutes later, well over the line at 12,000 feet, Biggles scanned the sky anxiously. Far away to the right, 3,000 feet above him, a formation of 'Fours**' were heading towards the line after a raid; he hoped that they would prove an attractive lure for any prowling enemy aircraft.

Ariet lay just ahead and below; Biggles put his nose down and dived, his eyes searching for his objective. Two miles west of Ariet, the Colonel had said! Good heavens, there seemed to be hundreds of oblong fields two miles west of Ariet. He looked at the photograph which he had pinned to his instrument board and compared it to the ground below. That must be the field, over there to the right. He spun to lose height more rapidly. Pulling out, he examined the field closely. An encampment seemed dangerously close—perhaps a mile away, not more. There was the field. He noticed two horses idling in a corner and looked anxiously at a row of poplars which stood like a row of soldiers at the far end. 'If I do get into that field I shall be mighty

---

* Slang: staff officers, (ie very senior officers), referring to the gold braid worn on their caps.
** De Havilland 4s—British two-seater day bomber 1917–1920. W. E. Johns flew a DH4 with 55 Squadron.

lucky to get out of it again,' he mused. Fortunately the wind—as the Colonel had said—was blowing in the right direction, otherwise it would be impossible.

He was only a couple of hundred feet up now and he could see men running about the encampment; some were clustered in little crouching groups, and as he cut his engine off he heard the faint rattle of a machine gun. He winced as something crashed through the fuselage behind him. 'That's too close,' he muttered, and in the same breath, 'Well, here goes.'

He did a swift S turn, then kicked out his left foot and brought the stick over in a steep side-slip. As he levelled out the tops of the trees brushed his undercarriage wheels and he fish-tailed* desperately to lose height.

The poplars at the far end of the field appeared to race towards him; he held his breath as his wheels touched the ground in a tail-wheel landing. 'A molehill now, and I somersault,' he thought, cursing himself for coming in so fast. His tail dropped, the skid dragged, and he breathed again. Without waiting for the machine to finish its run he swung round towards the tree in the corner. That must be the one, he thought. Springing quickly from the cockpit he looked around— ah! there was the rabbit-hole. He was on his hands and knees in a second, arms thrust far down. Nothing!

For a moment he remained stupefied with dismay. 'Must be another hole—or another tree,' he thought frantically, as he sprang to his feet. Realizing that he was on the verge of panicking, he steadied himself with an effort, and ran towards the next tree; his foot caught in an obstruction and he sprawled headlong, but he

---

* A quick side-to-side movement of the rudder, used when landing to reduce speed by creating extra wind resistance.

was on his feet again in an instant, instinctively glancing behind him to ascertain the cause of his fall. It was a rabbit-hole—there were a cluster of them all about him. Of course, there would be, he thought grimly, and thrust his hand into the nearest. Thank God! His fingers closed around a bulky object—he pulled it out—it was a thick packet of papers.

He raced towards the Camel. Two hundred yards away a file of soldiers with an officer at their head were coming at the double. He tossed the packet into the cockpit, swung himself into his seat, and the next instant was racing, tail up, down the field to get into the wind. His heart sank as he surveyed the poplars; they seemed to reach upwards to the sky. 'Can't be done,' he said, bitterly. In one place there was a gap in the line where a tree had fallen; could he get between them? He thought not, but he would try.

Already the grey-clad troops were scrambling through the hedge below the poplars. He opened the throttle and shoved the stick forward. The tail lifted. Hop—hop—thank goodness—she was off! He held his nose down for a moment longer and then zoomed at the middle of the gap. He flinched instinctively as a sharp crackling stabbed his ears and the machine shivered; whether it was gunshots or breaking wings, he didn't know.

He was through, in the air, and he'd got the plans! He laughed with relief as he dodged and twisted to spoil the aim of the marksmen below. Dare he waste time trying to gain height? He thought not. He would never be able to get to a safe height—better to stick at two or three thousand feet just out of range of small arms from the ground, race for home, and trust to luck. With every nerve vibrating he looked up, around and below; most of the time he flew with his head thrown back, searching the sky above and in front of him, the direction from which danger would come. Not a machine was in sight. Half-way home he had climbed to 4,000 feet; tail up, he raced for the line, swerving from time to time when archie came too close to be comfortable. Fortunately the wind had died away; ten minutes now would see him safe over the line. Ten minutes! A lot could happen in the air in ten minutes. His eyes were never still; anxiously they roved the air for signs of enemy aircraft, or for Mahoney or MacLaren's Camels.

Where was the packet? He groped about the floor of the cockpit, but couldn't find it. It must have got under his seat and drifted down the fuselage out of reach. Instinctively he glanced at the rev. counter. If he had to force-land now the enemy would find the packet. Would they! He felt for his Very* pistol and made sure that it was loaded. 'Provided I don't crash I can always set fire to her,' he reflected; 'the plans will burn with the rest.'

His eyes, still searching, suddenly stopped and focussed on a spot ahead. His heart missed a beat and his lips curled in a mirthless smile. Across the sky, straight ahead, moving swiftly towards him, were a line of straight-winged aeroplanes. Fokkers! Six of them.

He looked above the Fokkers for the expected Camels, but they were not there. 'All right,' muttered Biggles, 'I'll take the lot of you; come on, you devils.' For perhaps a minute they flew thus, the Camel, cut

---

* Short-barrelled pistol for firing coloured flares, used as a signal. Before the days of radio in aircraft different coloured flares were often used to pass messages.

off by the Fokkers, still heading for the line, with the distance rapidly closing between them.

'They'll get me, damn 'em; I can't fight that lot and get away with it,' thought Biggles. Even as the thought crossed his mind the enemy machines made a swift turn and started climbing for more height. A puzzled expression crossed Biggles' face as he watched the manœuvre. 'What's the big idea?' he muttered. 'They're making a lot of fuss about one poor solitary Camel. They behave as if they were scared of me.' Not since the first moment that he had spotted the enemy aircraft had Biggles taken his eyes off them; now, still following the Fokkers round, they stopped abruptly and he started with astonishment. Twenty feet away from his right-wing tip was a Camel. Mahoney, in the cockpit, pushed up his goggles and grinned derisively at him. Biggles looked to the left and saw another Camel; he recognized MacLaren's machine. He glanced behind him and saw two more Camels bringing up the rear.

Biggles almost felt himself turn pale. 'My God!' he breathed, 'where did they come from? And I never saw them. Am I going blind? Suppose they had been Fokkers, it would have been just the same except that I'd be smoking on the floor by now. No wonder the Fokkers swerved when they saw this lot coming. Five against six,' he mused, 'that's better. They'll come in now, but they'll have to be quick to stop us, it isn't four miles to home.' Already he could see the British balloon line.* 'Good old Mac, good old Mahoney,' he thought exultantly.

* Both sides in the First World War used kite or observation balloons, with observers in baskets suspended below the balloon, for spotting guns and enemy troop movements. Their slang name was gas bags or sausages.

The Fokkers were coming in now, the leader dropping on one of the rear Camels which swung round like a whirlwind and nosed up to face its attack head-on. The other Fokkers closely followed the first, and Mac and Mahoney turned outwards to meet them. Biggles' hand gripped the stick in a spasm of impotent rage at the realization that he would have to run for it and leave them to do his fighting for him. Twice he half-turned and checked himself. 'I'll never take on another job like this as long as I live,' he swore.

Two Fokker triplanes passed him to the eastward, making for the dog-fight now ranging behind him. He was low, and against the sun they had not seen him. Thrusting aside the temptation to take advantage of his ideal position for attack, Biggles raced across the line, swearing savagely to himself. He dare not trust himself to look back. Suppose they got Mac or Mahoney—he daren't think of it. Curse that brass-hat and his messenger-boy errands, anyway. Well, he was over the line now—safe—safe with his damned packet. As the aerodrome loomed up he shifted slightly in his seat for a better view. He moved his hand to shift a lump which seemed to have formed in the cushion on his seat and the lump came away in his hand. It was the packet. 'It must have fallen on the seat and I've been sitting on it all the time—too worried to notice it,' he laughed. Then he put his nose down and dived for the aerodrome; 100, 120, 150 ticked up on the speed indicator.

Major Mullen and Colonel Raymond were standing on the tarmac waiting for him; he could see the Colonel's red tabs. He took the joystick in his left hand and the packet in his right—100 feet—50 feet—30—he saw the Colonel duck as he flung the plans at him, and then, after a wild zoom, swung round in a climbing turn for the line.

As he neared the support trenches he saw three Camels coming towards him. He looked anxiously for Mahoney's blue propeller boss; it was not among them. 'They've got old Mahoney'—he swallowed a lump in his throat. The three Camels turned and fell in line with him. Mac, in the nearest, flew closer and waved his hand and jabbed downwards. Looking down Biggles saw a Camel with a smashed undercarriage standing crookedly among the shell holes. By its side was a figure waving cap and goggles. Mahoney! He must have been shot up and just made the line, thought Biggles, as, with joy in his heart, he turned for home.

The C.O. was waiting for him on the tarmac when he landed.

'Don't you know better than to throw things at staff officers?' he said smiling. 'The Colonel has dashed back to headquarters with your billet-doux; he has asked me to thank you and to say that he will not forget to-day's work.'

'You can tell him when you see him that I won't either,' grinned Biggles. 'Come on, chaps, let's go and fetch Mahoney, and finish that rubber.'

Chapter 3
J–9982

Biggles hummed contentedly to himself as he circled slowly at 16,000 feet. He looked at his watch; he had been out nearly two hours on a solitary patrol which had so far proved uneventful. 'I'll do another five minutes and then pack up,' he decided.

Below him lay a great bank of broken altocumulus cloud. Detached solid-looking masses of gleaming white mist floated languidly above the main cloud-bank. Not another plane was in the air, at least, not above the cloud, as far as he could see. Every few minutes he turned, and holding his hand before his eyes studied the glare in the direction of the sun long and carefully between extended fingers. If danger lurked anywhere it was from there that it would probably come. He examined the cloud-bank below in detail, section by section. His eyes fell on a Camel coming towards him, far below, threading its way between the broken masses of cloud through which the ground occasionally showed in a blur of bluey-grey.

Biggles placed himself between the sun and the other Camel as he watched it; it would pass about a thousand feet below. 'You poor hoot,' thought Biggles as he watched the machine disinterestedly. 'If I was a Fokker you'd be a dead man by now. Ah! here comes his partner.' The second Camel had emerged from the cloud-bank and was now rapidly overtaking the first. The pilot of the leading Camel was evidently wide-awake, for he turned back towards the second Camel and then circled to allow it to overtake him. Biggles noted that the second Camel was slightly above the leading one and that instead of putting its nose down to line up with it, the pilot was deliberately climbing for more height.

The second Camel was not more than fifty feet behind the first when its nose suddenly dropped as if the pilot intended to ram it. 'Silly ass,' thought Biggles; 'what fool's game is he playing? That's how accidents happen.' He caught his breath in amazed horror as a stream of tracers suddenly spurted from the guns of the topmost Camel point-blank into the cockpit of the one below. The stricken machine lurched drunkenly, a tongue of flame ran down the fuselage, its nose dropped and it dived through the cloud-bank out of sight, leaving only a little dark patch of smoke to mark its going.

For a moment Biggles stared unbelievingly, his brain refusing to believe what his eyes had seen.

'Great God!' he gasped, and then, thrusting the stick forward, he dived on the murderer out of the sun. But the other Camel was diving too, the pilot evidently intending to get below the cloud to watch the result of his handiwork. Biggles noted that the pilot did not once look up, and he was barely thirty feet behind it and slightly to one side when it disappeared into the swirling mist. Biggles pulled up to avoid a collision. 'J–9982,' he muttered aloud, naming the maker's number which he had seen painted in white letters on the fin of the diving machine. 'J–9982,' he repeated again. 'All right, you swine, I'll remember you.'

He circled for a moment and dived through a hole in the clouds, not daring to risk a collision in the opaque mist. He looked about him quickly as he pulled out below the cloud, but the Camel had disappeared. Far below he could see a long trail of black smoke where the fallen machine was still burning. For ten minutes he searched in vain, and then, feeling sick with rage and horror, he headed for the line. He wondered who was in the Camel which had been so foully attacked; he knew it must be either from his own or 231 Squadron, as they were the only Camel Squadrons in that area. He landed, and taxied quickly towards the sheds where a group of pilots lounged.

'Anybody out, Mac?' he almost snapped at MacLaren who had walked over to meet him.

'Yes, Mahoney's out with Forest and Hall on an O.P.*,' replied MacLaren, looking at him curiously. 'Here they come now,' he added, pointing to the sky in the direction of the line. 'Two of 'em, anyway.'

Biggles watched the two machines land, and Mahoney and Forest climbed out of their cockpits. 'Where's Hall, Mahoney?' he asked in a strained voice.

'About somewhere—won't be long I expect—he went fooling off on his own after I'd washed out,' answered the Flight-Commander.

'Towards Berniet?'

'Yes—why?'

'You can pack his kit—he won't be coming back,' said Biggles slowly, with a catch in his voice. He turned on his heel and walked towards the Squadron office.

Major Mullen smiled as he entered. 'Sit down, Biggles,' he said, the smile giving way to a look of anxiety as he noted the expression on the pilot's face.

'What's wrong, laddie?' he asked, coming quickly towards him.

* Offensive patrol, actively looking for something to attack.

44

Biggles told him what he'd seen, while the C.O. listened incredulously. 'Good heavens, Biggles,' he said at the end, 'what a hellish thing to do! What shall we do about it?'

'I am going over to 231 Squadron to see if they know anything about the other machine,' said Biggles shortly. 'It was never one of ours.'

'If it's a Hun we shall have to warn every Squadron along the line,' exclaimed Major Mullen gravely.

'And the Hun will know he is spotted within twenty-four hours,' sneered Biggles. 'You know what their intelligence service is like. At the first word he'll change the number on the machine and then we shall be in a hell of a mess. We have got him taped as it is, and he doesn't know it. No! You leave this to me, sir; we've got to take a chance. We'll get him, don't you worry.'

Twenty minutes later Biggles strode into the ante-room of 231 Squadron. A chorus of salutations, couched according to individual taste, greeted him. 'No, thanks, old man—can't stay now,' he replied curtly to a dozen invitations to have a drink.

'On the water waggon, Biggles?' asked Major Sharp, the C.O.

'No, sir, but I've got several things to do and I don't want to waste time. I have a word for your private ear, sir.'

'Certainly, what is it?' replied the Major at once.

'Have you got a Camel on your strength numbered J–9982?' inquired Biggles.

'I don't know, but Tommy will tell us. Tommy!' he called to the Equipment Officer, 'come here a minute. Do you happen to know if we have a machine numbered J–9982 on the station?'

'Not now, sir; but we had. That was Jackson's

45

machine; he went West at the beginning of the month, you remember.'

'Anybody see him crash?' asked Biggles.

'Don't think so, but I'll check up on the combat reports if you like. Speaking from memory, he went on a balloon-strafing show and never came back; yes, that was it.'

'So that was it, was it,' said Biggles slowly. 'Righto, Tommy, many thanks.'

Biggles took Major Sharp on one side and spoke to him earnestly for some minutes, the Major nodding his head as if in agreement from time to time.

'Right, sir,' he said at length, 'we'll leave it like that. Goodbye, sir. Cheerio, Tommy—cheerio, chaps,'

Major Mullen looked up as Biggles re-entered his office.

'It was as I thought, sir,' began Biggles. 'A Hun is flying that kite.'

'I can't believe a German pilot would do such a dastardly thing,' said the Major, shaking his head.

'No ordinary officer would, of course,' agreed Biggles, 'I'll bet you anything you like he is in no regular squadron. None of the Richthofen Staffel* would stand for that stuff any more than we would. But you'll find skunks in every mob if you look for 'em. The higher command wouldn't stand in a chap's way if he was low enough to do it. Maybe they've detailed somebody for the job for a special reason; you can never tell. One thing is certain. The pilots over the

* German equivalent of a squadron, 12 or 13 planes which fly together, often named after their leader, as here, where it is named after Baron Von Richthofen 'The Red Baron' the top scoring World War One fighter pilot, who shot down 80 Allied planes, before being killed in 1918.

46

other side know all about it or they'd shoot him down themselves. He's got a private mark somewhere. The archie batteries must know it, too. He drops them a light or throws some stunt occasionally so that they'll know it's him and not open fire.'

'I shall have to report it to Wing,' said the Major seriously.

'Give me forty-eight hours, sir,' begged Biggles, 'and then you can do what you like. Report it to Wing, and it will be known from Paris to Berlin and from Calais to Switzerland before the day's out. There won't be one Hun flying a Camel. Every Camel our archie batteries see will have a Hun in it, and they'll shoot at it. We'll be a blight in the sky—a target for every other pilot in the air to shoot at. A pretty mess that would be. Perhaps that is what the Huns are hoping for. Stand on what I tell you, sir; forget it for twenty-four hours, anyway, and you won't regret it. I'm going to talk to Mac and Mahoney, then I'm going over to look for him. I know his hunting-ground. I just want to see him once more—just once—through my sights.' Biggles, breathing heavily, departed to look for the other Flight Commanders.

He found them in the sheds and called them aside. 'Listen, chaps,' he began, 'there's a Hun flying a Camel over the line. His number is J–9982. J—9—9—8—2, remember it. If you let your imagination play on that for a moment you'll realize just what that means. We've got to get him, and get him quick. It was he who got Hall—I saw him, the dirty cannibal.'

MacLaren turned pale as death. Mahoney, his Celtic temper getting the better of him, spat a burst of profanity. His rage brought tears to his eyes.

47

'Well,' said Biggles, 'that's that, and it's enough; I'm going to look for him. You coming?'

'We're coming,' said the two pilots together, grimly.

'All right, now look, we've got to be careful. You can't shoot at a Camel like you would at a Hun. I'm going to paint my prop boss, centre-section and fin, blue. Sharp is painting all 231 Squadron machines like that so we'll know 'em. He knows the reason, but none of his officers do. None of our fellows are leaving the ground until we come back. If you see a Camel *without* these markings it may be him. If he is over Hunland and not being archied, it's almost certain to be him; but look for the number on the fin before you shoot. J–9982. If you see a Camel wearing that number, shoot quick and ask questions afterwards. He was working over the Berniet sector when I saw him, and that is where I am going to look for him. I'm off now.'

The sun was low in the western sky; Biggles, patrolling at 14,000 feet, yawned. Lord! he was tired. This was his fourth patrol; he seemed to have been in the sky all day—looking for a Camel without a blue prop-boss. He had seen MacLaren and Mahoney several times; they too were still searching. Biggles had found a Hanoverana* and shot it down in flames at the first burst without satisfying the stone-cold desire to kill which consumed him. He had been attacked by three Tripe-hounds** and had returned the attack with such savage fury and good effect that they acknowledged their mistake by diving for home.

This should have improved his temper, but it did

* German two-seater fighter and ground attack biplane.
** Slang: German fighter with three wings on each side, with two forward-firing guns.

not. Biggles wanted a certain Camel, and nothing would satisfy him until he had seen it plunging earthwards in flames, like its victim. He almost hoped that neither Mac nor Mahoney would find it and rob him of the pleasure. Biggles yawned again; he could hardly keep awake, he was so tired. 'This won't do,' he muttered, and leaned out of the cockpit to let the icy slipstream fan his cheeks. Three black spots appeared in front of him and he had warmed his guns before he realized that they were only oil spots on his goggles. He wiped them clean and for the hundredth time began a systematic scrutiny of the atmosphere in every direction.

It would be dark in half an hour. Already the earth was a vast swell of blue and purple shadows. 'It's a washout,' he thought bitterly. 'I might as well be getting home; he's gone to roost.' Without losing height he commenced a wide circle towards his own lines; his eye fell on a tiny speck far over and heading still farther in over the British lines. Small as it was, he recognized it for a Camel. 'Mac or Mahoney going home, I expect,' he said to himself; 'well, I'll just make one more cast.' The outer edge of his circle took him well over enemy lines, and ignoring the usual salvo of archie he looked long and searchingly into the enemies' country. A cluster of black spots attracted his attention. He recognized it for German archie and flew closer to ascertain the reason for it. 'S' turning, he climbed steadily and kept his eye on the bursts. He could see two machines approaching now, and the straight top wings and dihedral-angled lower planes told him they were Camels. A minute later he could see that both had blue prop-bosses. Mac and Mahoney!

Suddenly he stiffened in his seat. Who was it then

that he had seen far over his own lines? He was round in a flash heading for the direction taken by the lone machine. Five minutes later he saw a machine coming towards him. It was a Camel! His heart thumping uncomfortably with excitement, Biggles circled cautiously to meet it. His nostrils quivered when he was close enough to see that the prop-boss was unpainted and the leading edge of the centre-section was painted brown. An icy hand seemed to clutch his heart. Suppose he made a mistake! Suppose it was one of his own boys—out without order—he daren't think about it.

The Camel was close now, the pilot waving a greeting, but Biggles' eyes were fixed on the fin. J-.... the numbers seemed to run into each other. Was he going blind? He pushed up his goggles and looked again. J–9982, he read, and grated his teeth.

The Camel closed up until it was flying beside him; the pilot smiling. Biggles showed his teeth in what he imagined to be an answering smile. 'You swine,' he breathed: 'you dirty, unutterable, murdering swine! I'm going to kill you if it's the last thing I do on earth.' Something made him glance upwards. Five Fokker triplanes were coming down on him like bolts from the blue. 'So, that's it, is it?' he muttered. 'You're the bait and I'm the fish. That's your game. Well, they'll get me, but you're getting yours first.'

Swiftly he moved the stick slightly back, sideways, and then forwards. 'Hold that, you rat,' he shouted, as he pressed his triggers. Rat-tat-tat-tat-tat-tat-tat-tat— a double stream of glittering tracer poured into the false Camel's cockpit. The pilot slumped forward in his seat and the machine nosed downwards.

Beside himself with rage, Biggles followed it, the Fokkers forgotten. 'Hold that—AND THAT'—he gritted through his teeth as he poured in burst after burst at point-blank range. 'Burn, you hound!' He laughed aloud as a streamer of yellow fire curled aft along the side of the fuselage. The rattle of guns near at hand made him look over his shoulder; a Fokker was on his tail, Spandaus stuttering. Another Fokker roared past with a Camel apparently glued to its tail; and still another Fokker and Camel were circling in tight spirals above. 'Go to it, boys,' grinned Biggles as he pulled the joystick right back into his stomach, and half-rolling off the top of the loop looked swiftly for the Fokker that had singled him out for destruction. Rat-tat-tat-tat . . . 'Oh! there you are,' he muttered, as the Fokker, which had followed his manœuvre, came at him again. Biggles, fighting mad, flew straight at it, guns streaming lead; the German lost his nerve first and swerved, Biggles swinging round on its tail, guns still going. Without warning, the black-crossed machine seemed to go to pieces in the air, and Biggles turned to look for the others. He saw a Camel spinning—a Tripehound followed it down. He thrust his joystick forward and poured in a long burst at the Fokker, which, turning like lightning and nearly standing on its tail, spat a stream of death at him. It stalled as Biggles zoomed over it.

Where were the others? Biggles looked around for the Camel he had seen spinning and breathed a sigh of relief when he saw it far below streaking for the line. A Fokker was smoking on the ground near the false Camel. Then he discovered another Camel flying close behind him. For the first time since the combat began he realized it was nearly dark. Feeling suddenly limp from reaction he waved to his companion, and together they dived for the line, emptying their guns into the

51

enemy trenches as they passed over. The Camel below had already crossed the line to safety.

Major Mullen was waiting anxiously for them when they landed.

'Have you been balloon-strafing, Biggles?' he asked, looking aghast at bullet-shattered struts and torn fabric.

'No, sir,' replied Biggles with mock dignity, 'but I have to report that I have today shot down a British aircraft numbered J–9982, recently on the strength of 231 Squadron, and more recently the equipment of an enemy pilot, name unknown.'

He broke into a peal of nerve-jarring laughter which ended in something like a sob. 'Get me a drink somebody, please,' he pleaded. 'Lord! I am tired.'

Chapter 4
The Balloonatics

Captain James Bigglesworth brought the Headquarters car to a halt within a foot of the Service tender which had just stopped outside the Restaurant Chez Albert in the remote village of Clarmes. As he stepped out of the car, Captain Wilkinson of 287 Squadron leapt lightly from the tender. Biggles eyed him with astonishment.

'Hullo, Wilks!' he cried. 'What the deuce brings you here?'

'What are you doing here?' parried Wilkinson.

'I've come'—Biggles paused—'I've come to do some shopping,' he said brightly.

'What a funny thing, so have I,' grinned Wilkinson, 'and as I was here first I'm going to be served first. You've missed the boat, Biggles.'

'I'm dashed if I have,' cried Biggles hotly. 'Our crowd discovered it—you pull your stick back, Wilks, and let the dog see the rabbit.'

'Not on your life,' retorted Wilkinson briskly. 'First come, first served. You go and aviate your perishing Camel.' So saying he made a swift dash for the door of the estaminet; but he was not quite fast enough. Biggles tackled him low, brought him down with a crash, and together they rolled across the sun-baked earth.

Just how the matter would have ended it is impossible to say, but at that moment a touring car pulled up beside them with a grinding of brakes and Colonel Raymond, of Wing Headquarters, eyed the two belligerent officers through a monocle with well-feigned astonishment.

'Gentlemen! Officers! No, I must be mistaken,' he said softly, but with a deadly sarcasm that brought a blush to the cheeks of both officers. 'Are there no enemy aircraft left in the air that you must bicker among yourselves on the high road? Come, come. Can I be of any assistance?' He left the car, bade his chauffeur drive on, and came towards them. 'Now,' he said sternly, 'what is all this about?'

'That is the point, sir,' began Biggles. 'Yesterday morning Batty—that is, Batson, of my Flight—was coming back this way by road from a forced landing, and dropped in here for—er—well, I suppose, for a drink. During a conversation with the proprietor he learned that M. Albert had, some years ago, laid in a stock of whisky at the request of the staff of an Englishman who had taken the Château d'Abnay for the season. When this man returned to England, Albert had some of the stuff left on his hands, and, as the local bandits do not apparently drink whisky, it is still here. To make a long story short, sir, Batty—that is, Batson—found no less than fourteen bottles of the pre-War article reposing under the cobwebs in the cellar—and going for the pre-War price of five francs fifty the bottle. Unfortunately Batty—I mean Batson—had only enough money on him to bring one bottle back to the Mess, so I slipped along this morning to get the rest. But it appears that Batty—that is, Batson—went to a binge—er—guest night—at 287 Squadron last night and babbled the good news—at least that is presumably what happened since I find Captain Wilkinson here this morning. I think you will agree, sir, that having been found by an officer of 266 Squadron the stuff should rightly belong to them,' concluded Biggles, eyeing the would-be sharer of the spoils in cold anger.

'Well, well,' said the Colonel after a brief pause, 'if that is the cause of the trouble I can settle the matter for you. The whisky has gone.'

'Gone!' cried Biggles aghast—'all of it?'

'Yes, I fear so,' replied the Colonel sadly.

'Can you understand the mentality of a man who would take the lot and leave none for anyone else,' exclaimed Biggles bitterly. 'Do you know who it was, sir?'

The Colonel paused for a moment before replying. 'Well, as a matter of fact, it was me,' he admitted, the corners of his mouth twitching.

Biggles turned red and then white. Wilkinson started a guffaw which he turned to a cough as the Colonel's eye fell on him.

'You see,' went on the Colonel, 'I, too, was a guest at 287 Squadron Mess last night, and fearing that the whisky might fall into unappreciative hands, I collected it on my way home. I have just come to pay for it.'

Biggles breathed heavily, but said nothing. Colonel Raymond eyed him sympathetically, and then brightened as an idea struck him.

'Now, I'll be fair about this; I'll tell you what I'll do,' he began.

'I know! Toss for it, sir,' suggested Biggles eagerly, feeling in his pocket for a coin.

The Colonel shook his head. 'No,' he said, 'I've a better idea than that; do you fellows know the Duneville balloon?'

Biggles showed his teeth in a mirthless smile. 'Do I? I should say I do! When I'm tired of life I am going to fly within half a mile of that sausage. That's all that will be necessary.'

Wilkinson nodded. 'You won't have to go so far as that, Biggles,' he said. 'Go within a mile of that kite and you'll see old man Death waiting with the door wide open.'

'In that case it doesn't 'matter,' said the Colonel, preparing to enter the estaminet.

'Just a moment, sir! What about the balloon?' cried Biggles anxiously.

'Well, what I was going to suggest was this,' replied the Colonel. 'Strictly between ourselves, the infantry are doing a show in the morning. We are moving a lot of troops, and that observation balloon has got to come down and stay down. I'm willing to hand over six bottles of that whisky, free, gratis and for nothing, to the officer who does most to keep that balloon on the floor for the next few hours. To-day is Sunday. Time expires twelve noon to-morrow. We'll score like this. Forcing the ground crew to haul the balloon down counts three points; shooting it down in flames, five points. My observers will have their glasses on the balloon all day. You know as well as I do that if you shoot the balloon down there will be another one up within a few hours. Duneville is an important observation post for the Boche.'

'Did you say just now that you would be *fair*, sir?' asked Biggles incredulously.

Colonel Raymond ignored the thrust. 'Pulled down—a try—three points; down in flames—goal—five points; don't forget.' In the doorway of the estaminet he turned and a broad smile spread over his face. 'Any officer taking the balloon prisoner scores a grand slam and gets the other six bottles. Good-bye.'

For a full minute the two Flight-Commanders stood staring at the closed door as if fascinated; then Biggles started towards his car. With his foot on the running-board he turned to Wilkinson.

'You keep your damned glasshouse out of my way,' he said curtly, referring to the S.E.5, which was, at that time, fitted with a semi-cabin windscreen.

'And you keep your oil-swilling "hump" where it belongs,' snapped Wilkinson, referring to Biggles' Camel.

Inside the estaminet Colonel Raymond was sipping pre-War whisky with the air of a connoisseur; Albert was packing twelve bottles into a case. 'Unless I am very much mistaken,' mused the Colonel, 'that Boche balloon is in for a trying time—a very trying time.'

An hour later Biggles, clad in a leather coat, made his way towards the hangars. In his pocket he carried written orders to strafe the Duneville Balloon; these orders permitted him to carry Buckingham (incendiary) bullets, forbidden on pain of death for any other purpose by the rules of war. Rules were seldom observed during the great struggle, but the order would, at least, protect him from trouble at the hands of the enemy, should he be forced to land on the wrong side of the lines. He halted before a Camel upon which a squad of ack-emmas were working feverishly.

'What are you doing, Flight?' he asked the Flight-Sergeant in charge.

'Just a top overhaul, sir, while you were away,' replied the Flight-Sergeant. 'She'll be ready in an hour.'

Biggles frowned, but said nothing; he was disappointed to find his machine wasn't ready, but he would not say anything to discourage the mechanics. 'Fill the belts with tracer and Buckingham right through in that order,' he said presently as he seated himself and prepared to wait.

'Going balloon strafing, sir?' Biggles nodded. The Sergeant shrugged his shoulders and said no more.

The machine was ready at last. Biggles, fretting with impatience, took off and headed for the line, climbing all the time in the direction of Duneville. It did not take him many minutes to spot his objective. There it was, the mis-shapen beast, four miles away and five thousand feet below him. Circling cautiously towards it he examined the air and ground in its vicinity carefully. He could see nothing, but he knew perfectly well that once let him venture within a mile of that sausage floating so placidly in the blue vault, the air about it would be a maelstrom of fire and hurtling metal. He started. Far above the balloon appeared a tiny black speck surrounded by a halo of black smoke and little darting jabs of flame. Biggles swore and raced towards the scene, watching the machine which he now recognized as an S.E.5, with interest. 'Sweet spirits of nitre,' he muttered, 'What a hell to be flying through, all for a case of whisky. He must be crazy.' The S.E.5 was going down in an almost vertical dive, twisting like a wounded sparrow-hawk, pieces of torn fabric streaming out behind it. Swift as had been its descent the balloon crew were faster, and the sausage was on the ground before the S.E. could reach it. The machine pulled up in an almost vertical zoom, and as it flew past him, Wilkinson, the pilot, pushed up his goggles and then very deliberately, jabbed up three fingers at him.

'Three points, eh,' muttered Biggles. He placed his

thumb against his nose and extended his fingers in the time-honoured manner. Wilkinson grinned, and with a parting wave, turned for home. Biggles climbed away disconsolately.

For an hour he circled around, returning at intervals to see if the balloon had reappeared, but there was no sign of it, and he knew the reason. 'They can see me,' he pondered. 'They know why I'm hanging around; presently they'll send for a Staffel of Huns to drive me away. I'll have to try different tactics.' He returned to the aerodrome, refuelled, and returning to the line crossed over four or five miles from the balloon station. For ten minutes he flew straight into the enemies' country and then circled back to approach the balloon from its own side of the line. Looking ahead anxiously, his heart leapt as his eyes fell on the ungainly gas-bag floating below him. Instinctively he looked upwards to make sure that there were no protecting machines, and caught his breath sharply.

Three Fokker Triplanes were coming down in a steep dive, but not in his direction. Following their line of flight he saw an S.E.5 which, apparently, just realizing its danger was streaking for home. 'That's Wilks,' thought Biggles, 'Wilks for a certainty. He did the same thing as I've done and was just going for the sausage when he saw them coming. They'll get him. They've 3,000 feet of height on him—he'll never reach the line. The Tripehounds have left the coast clear for me though; I'll never get such a chance again. It's Wilks or the balloon—damn the luck—I can't let them get old Wilks.' He put his nose down in the wake of the Fokkers in a wire-screaming dive.

He reached the nearest Fokker almost at the same time as the leading Fokker fired at the S.E.; at that moment the black-crossed machines were too intent on their quarry to look back. Biggles held his fire until his propeller was only a few feet from the nearest enemy machine, and then raked it from tail skid to propeller-boss with one deadly burst. The Triplane slowly turned over on to its back. Hearing the shots, the other two Fokkers whirled round, leaving the S.E. a clear run home. Biggles, cold as ice, was on the tail of the nearest in a flash, and the next instant all three machines were turning in a tight circle. The Fokkers started to outclimb him at once, as he knew they would. 'I'm in a mess now,' he muttered, as the top Fokker levelled out to come down on him, and he pulled the Camel up to take it head-on.

What was that? An S.E.5 was above them all, coming down like a comet on the Fokker, guns streaming two pencil lines of white smoke. The Fokker turned and dived, the S.E. on its tail. 'Good for you, Wilks,' grinned Biggles; 'that evens things up.' He looked for the other Triplane, but it was a mile away far over its own side of the line.

Then he remembered the balloon. Where was it? Great Scott! there it was, still up, less than a mile away. Even as Biggles put his nose down towards it, its crew seemed to divine his intention and started to haul it down. A stabbing flame and a cloud of black smoke appeared in front of him, but he did not alter his course. He was flying through a hail of archie and machine gun bullets now, every nerve taut, eyes on the blurred mass of the balloon. Five hundred feet—three hundred—one hundred, the distance closed between them: 'At least I won't be out for a duck,' he muttered as he pressed his triggers. He had a fleeting vision of the observers' parachutes opening as they sprang from

60

the basket, a great burst of flame, and then he was twisting upwards in a wild zoom in the direction of the line.

He breathed a sigh of relief as he passed over. An S.E.5 appeared by his side, the pilot waving a greeting. Biggles pulled off his gauntlet and jabbed five fingers upwards. 'There will be no more balloons to-day,' he said to himself, glancing towards the setting sun, as he made for home.

As he landed, 'Wat' Tyler, the Recording Officer, handed him a slip. 'Signal for you from Wing, just in,' he said. 'Damned if I know what it means.'

Biggles glanced at the message and grinned. 'Score 5–3 your favour,' he read. The initials were those of Colonel Raymond.

'Tired of life, Biggles?'

Biggles looked up from the combat report to see Major Mullen eyeing him sadly.

'Why, sir?' he asked.

'You've been balloon strafing,' said the C.O.

'That's true, sir, I had a little affair with the Duneville sausage this afternoon,' admitted Biggles.

'I see,' said the C.O. 'Well, if you're in a hurry to write yourself off*, go right ahead. You get balloon fever and you won't last a week; you know that as well as I do. Don't be a fool, Biggles, let 'em alone. By the way, I see that the wind has shifted; blowing straight over our way for a change. All right, finish your report,

---

* 'Write-off.' An aeroplane that was so badly damaged as to be of no further use was officially 'written-off' the squadron books. The expression 'write off' was loosely used to infer the complete destruction of anything.

but let those infernal kites alone,' he added, as he left the room.

Biggles remained with his pen poised, as an idea flashed into his mind. The wind was blowing straight over our lines, was it? He hurried to the window and looked at the wind-stocking. 'Lord! so it is,' he muttered, and sat down, deep in thought. What was it Colonel Raymond had said? 'Anybody capturing the balloon scores a grand slam and gets the other six bottles.' 'Great Scott!' he grinned, 'I wonder if it's possible? If I could cut the cable the balloon would drift over to our side. Cables have been cut by shell splinters before to-day. I wonder—!'

He dashed off to the nearest balloon squadron and after spending half an hour asking many questions in the company of a balloon officer, returned to the aerodrome still deep in thought. He sought his Flight-Sergeant.

'What bombs have we, Flight?' he asked.

'Only 20 lb. Coopers, sir,' replied the N.C.O.*, looking at him queerly.

'Nothing bigger?'

'No, sir.'

'I see. Do you think my Camel would carry a 112-pounder?' asked Biggles.

'Carry it all right, sir, if you could get a rack fixed, though you wouldn't be able to throw the machine about much with that lot on,' grinned the Flight-Sergeant.

'Where can we get one?'

'297 Squadron at Arville use them on their "Nines",

---

* Non Commissioned officer eg a Corporal or a Sergeant.

sir. If you gave me a chit to the E.O.* I could get one and borrow a bomb-rack.'

'Will you do that for me, Flight—and get it fixed to-night. I'm leaving the ground at daylight in the morning. I'd like a five-seconds delay fuse fixed, if you can manage it.'

'I'll have a shot at it, sir.'

Well satisfied with his evening's work, Biggles went to bed early.

At the first streak of dawn Biggles was in the cockpit warming up his engine. The Flight-Sergeant, as good as his word, had hung the bomb under the fuselage just clear of the undercarriage. The change of wind had brought low cloud and Biggles looked at it anxiously. Too much cloud would spoil visibility and the balloon would not go up.

The Camel took a long run to lift its unusual load, but once in the air the difference was hardly noticeable except for a slight heaviness on the controls. 'This is the maddest thing I've ever done in my life,' soliloquized the pilot, as he sped towards the lines. 'If I get away with it I'll sign the pledge.' As he approached Duneville he saw the balloon just going up, but following his tactics of the previous day he circled, crossed the line a few miles lower down, and prepared to attack from the German side. The balloon was straight ahead of him now and Biggles swore as his eye fell on a solitary S.E.5 farther west, trailing a line of archie bursts in its wake. Biggles put the nose of the Camel down and started hedge hopping** in the direction of the sausage, now far above him. Vaguely he heard the

* Equipment Officer.
** Flying very close to the ground, avoiding obstacles.

crackle of machine gun fire as he raced across the enemy reserve trenches, but he heeded it not. He was afraid of one thing only, and that was accidentally hitting the balloon cable with his wing; it was only about as thick as his finger and would be difficult to see. The balloon was less than a mile away now, the ground party no doubt looking upwards for any possible danger. With his wheels nearly touching the ground he tore towards the little group at the foot of the cable. He saw them turn in his direction, scatter and dive for shelter, and then he was on them. At the last instant he threw the machine in a bank away from the cable drum, pulled the bomb-toggle, and zoomed, twisting and turning as he dashed towards his own lines. As he reached comparative safety he looked back over his shoulder; a great pillar of smoke marked the spot where the bomb had burst, but the sausage was nowhere in sight.

Ignoring the archie that still followed him, Biggles pushed up his goggles and looked again, an expression of incredulous amazement on his face. A movement far above caught his eye and caused him to look up; an ejaculation of astonishment escaped his lips. The balloon, freed from its anchor, had shot up to ten or eleven thousand feet and was already sailing over no-man's-land! He could see no parachutes, and concluded that the observers, taken unawares, were still in the basket. Far away he saw an S.E.5 diving across the line to where the balloon would normally be. Biggles grinned. 'The bird has flown,' he muttered, as the S.E. pilot swung round in obvious confusion, evidently at a loss to know what had become of it, but when he began climbing, Biggles knew that his balloon had been sighted by the lynx-eyed Flight-Commander.

Biggles reached the balloon first, waved a greeting to the occupants who were busy with something inside the basket, and then fired a warning Very light in the direction of the rapidly approaching S.E.5. The Camel pilot guessed what had happened to the balloon. When the mooring cable had been cut it had shot up until the automatic valve had functioned, and, by releasing the gas, checked the ascent, and incidentally prevented the balloon from bursting. The observers had been too startled to take to their parachutes immediately, and then, seeing that they would in any case drift across the line and be taken prisoners, decided to remain where they were and bring their unwieldy craft to earth.

They were now opening the valve and losing height rapidly, which was exactly what Biggles had hoped would happen. He knew little of ballooning, but enough to understand what the two men in the basket would do. The balloon would drop with increasing rapidity; near the ground the crew would check its descent by throwing ballast overboard and then pull the rip-panel, releasing all the gas from the envelope, which would then collapse and sink lightly to earth. It happened as Biggles anticipated. Close to the ground the fabric spread out like a great mushroom and quietly settled down. Biggles landed in the next field, the S.E.5 landing a moment later. A touring car intercepted them as they crossed the road separating them from the deflated monster. Colonel Raymond greeted them.

'Who did that?' he laughed, pointing towards the balloon.

'My prisoner, sir,' grinned Biggles. 'I claim a grand slam and the twelve bottles. There will be no more balloons up at Duneville to-day.'

'You've won them,' laughed the Colonel. 'Collect them at the Chez Albert. They are paid for.'

'At the where?' said the two pilots together, staring. 'Do you mean to tell us that the whisky was in there all the time?' asked Biggles, with a marked lack of respect.

'Never mind,' said the Colonel soothingly, 'you'll be able to get marvellously drunk to-night.'

'Me! Drunk!' said Biggles disgustedly, 'I never drink whisky.'

Colonel Raymond looked at him in amazement. 'Then why—'

'You see, it's 266 guest-night to-morrow, and I thought we'd give everyone a treat. Will you come, sir? You will, Wilks, I know.'

'You bet I will!' cried both officers together.

Chapter 5
The Blue Devil

The summer sun shone down from a sky of cloudless blue. Biggles sat on the doorstep of No. 287 Squadron Mess and watched the evolutions of an aeroplane high overhead with puzzled interest, wondering what the pilot was trying to do.

He was on his way home from an uneventful morning patrol and had dropped in to have a word or two with Wilkinson, only to be told that he was in the air.

Slightly torpid from two hours at 16,000 feet he had settled down in the ante-room to await his return, when the amazing aerobatics of the S.E.5 above had attracted his attention. With several other officers he had moved to the door in order to obtain an uninterrupted view of the performance.

'That's Wilks all right,' observed Barrett, a comparative veteran of six months at the front. 'He's been doing that on and off for the last two days.'

Biggles nodded wonderingly. 'What's the matter with him?' he asked. 'I always thought he was crazy — just look at the fool, he'll break that machine in a minute.'

The evolutions of the S.E.5 were certainly sufficiently unusual to call for comment. The pilot appeared to be trying to do something between a vertical bank and a half-roll. Over and over he repeated the same manœuvre, sometimes falling out of it into a spin and sometimes in a stall.

'Here he comes, you can ask him,' said Barrett, as the engine was cut off and the S.E.5 commenced to glide down to land.

Biggles strolled across the tarmac to meet the pilot.

'How did that look from the ground?' asked Wilkinson, grinning, as he clambered out of the cockpit.

'It looked to me that if you were trying to strip the wings off that kite you must have damn nearly succeeded,' replied Biggles. 'Are you tired of life or something? What's the big idea, anyway?'

'Come across to the mess and I'll tell you,' answered Wilkinson, and together they made their way towards the ante-room.

'Now tell me this,' continued the S.E.5 pilot when they had called for drinks and made themselves comfortable, 'have you ever bumped into that blue and yellow Boche circus* that hangs out somewhere near Lille? I believe they are now on Aerodrome 27.'

'Too true I have,' admitted Biggles. 'What about them?'

'Have you seen 'em lately?'

'No! Come on, cough it up, laddie. Have they turned pink, or what?'

'No, they're still blue, but they've got a new leader, and if you place any value at all on your young life, keep out of his way, that's all,' replied Wilkinson soberly.

'Hot stuff, eh?' inquired Biggles.

'He's hotter than hell at twelve noon on midsummer's day,' declared Wilkinson. 'Now, let me tell you something else. First of all, as you know, these

---

* Slang: a formation of German fighter aircraft nicknamed circus by RFC pilots because of the Germans' brightly painted aircraft.

Albatroses* are all painted blue, but there's a bit of yellow on them somewhere.'

'Yes, I've noticed that,' replied Biggles, 'one of them has got yellow elevators, and there's another with a yellow centre-section.'

'That's right,' agreed Wilkinson. 'They've all got that touch of yellow on them somewhere, that is, all except the leader. That's what I'm told by one or two fellows who have seen him and lived to tell the tale. He's blue all over—no yellow anywhere. Blue propeller-boss, wheel discs, everything in fact. That marks him for you. The Huns call him the Blue Devil and they say he's got thirty machines in two months—every machine he's ever tackled. That's pretty good going, and, if it's true, he must be pretty smart. The most amazing thing about it is, though, they say his machine has never been touched by a bullet.'

'Who says?' inquired Biggles curiously.

'Wait a minute, don't be in such an infernal hurry. Now, until a couple of days ago we had only heard rumours about this bloke, but last Thursday I got one of his men, an N.C.O. pilot. I met him over Paschendale and we had a rough house; in the end I got his engine. For once the wind was blowing our way and we had drifted a bit in the scrap. To cut a long story short, he landed under control behind our lines. He managed to set fire to his machine before anybody could get to him, but we brought him back to the mess for a binge—you know. We made a wild night of it and under the influence of alcohol he started bragging, like a Boche will when he's had a few beers. Among other things he told us that this Blue Bird is going to knock

* German single-seater fighter with two fixed machine guns synchronised to fire through the propeller.

down every one of our machines one after the other, just like that. Now listen to this. This Hun has got a new stunt which sounds like the Immelmann business all over again. You remember that when Immelmann first invented his turn, nobody could touch him until we rumbled it, and then McCubbin got him. Everybody does the stunt now, so it doesn't cut much ice. Nobody knows quite what this new Hun does or how he does it. He's tried to explain it to his own chaps, but they can't get the hang of it, which seems damn funny, I'll admit. This lad I got tried to tell me how it was done when he was blotto—that is, the stick and rudder movements, but I couldn't follow how it worked. I've tried to do it in the air; you saw me trying just now. It's a new sort of turn; just when you get on this fellow's tail and kid yourself you've got him cold, he pivots somehow on his wing-tip and gets you. This lad of mine swore that the man who gets on his tail is cold meat—dead before he knows what's hit him. It sounds damned unlikely to me, but then the Immelmann turn probably sounded just as unlikely in its day. Well, that's the story, laddie, and now you know as much about it as I do. The point is, what are we going to do about it?'

Biggles pondered for a few moments. 'The thing seems to be for us to find him and see how he does it,' he observed in a flash of inspiration.

'I thought you'd get a rush of blood to the brain,' sneered Wilkinson. 'You get on his tail and I'll do the watching.'

'Funny, aren't you?' retorted Biggles. 'If I meet him I'll do my own watching and then come back and tell you all about it. Maybe you'll be able to earn your pay and get a Hun or two occasionally. Blue devils go pop at the end, if I remember my fireworks.'

On his way home Biggles thought a good deal about what Wilkinson had told him concerning the blue Albatros. 'Sooner or later I shall meet him,' he reflected, 'so I might as well decide how am I going to act. When he pulls this patent stunt he must reckon on the fellow he's fighting doing the usual thing, making a certain move at a certain time, and up to the present the fellow has always obliged him; but if he happened to do something else, something unorthodox, it might put him off his stroke. Well, we'll see; but it's difficult to know what to do if you don't know what the other fellow's going to do. If I could see the trick once I should know, but apparently he takes care that nobody gets a second chance.'

His curiosity prompted him to spend a good deal of time in the Lille area, but his vigilance was unrewarded; of the blue circus he saw no sign. He saw Wilkinson several times, and each time he learned that the Blue Devil had claimed another victim, but the knowledge only sharpened his curiosity.

By the perversity of fate it so happened that the encounter occurred at a moment when no thought of it was in his mind. He was returning from a lone patrol at 15,000 feet, deliberating in his mind as to whether or not he should have a shot at the new Duneville balloon as he crossed the lines, when his ever-watchful eye saw a grey shadow flit across a cloud far below. It was only a fleeting glimpse, but it was sufficient. It was not his own shadow. What, then? More from instinct than actual thought he whirled round and flung stick and rudder-bar hard over as the rattle of guns struck his ears. An Albatros screamed past him barely twenty feet away. 'Nearly caught me napping, did you?' muttered Biggles, as he swung the Camel in the wake of the enemy machine. He was on its tail in a flash, and only then did he notice its colour.

It was blue! Biggles caught his breath as he ran his eyes swiftly over it, looking for a touch of yellow, but there was none. 'So it's you, is it?' he muttered, as he tore after it, trying vainly to bring his sights to bear. 'Well, let's see the trick.'

He was as cold as ice, every nerve braced taut as a piece of elastic, for unless rumour lied, he was up against a foeman of outstanding ability, a man who had downed thirty machines in as many duels without once having his own machine touched.

Biggles knew that he was about to fight the battle of his life where one false move would mean the end. Neither of them had ever been beaten, but now one of them must taste defeat. In a few minutes either a Camel or an Albatros would be hurtling downwards on its way to oblivion. He tightened his grip on the joystick and warmed his guns with a short burst.

Both machines were banking vertically now, one each side of a circle not a hundred feet across. Round and round they raced as if swinging on an invisible pivot, the circle slowly decreasing in size. Tighter and tighter became the spiral as each pilot tried to see the other through his sights. The wind screamed in his wires and Biggles began to feel dizzy with the strain; he had lost all count of time and space, and of the perpendicular. His joystick was right back in his thigh as he strove to cut across a chord of the circle and place himself in a position for a shot. Always just in front of his nose was the blue tail, just out of range, just far enough in front to make shooting a waste of ammunition. Another few inches would do it; the ring of his sight cut across the blue tail now—God—just for a little more—just another inch. 'Come on, where's your trick?' snarled Biggles, feeling that he was getting giddy.

He was ready for it when it happened, although just how it came about he could never afterwards tell. At one moment his sights were within a foot of the blue cockpit; he saw the Boche turn his head slowly, and the next instant the blue nose was pointing at him, a double stream of scarlet flame pouring from the twin Spandau guns.

Biggles knew that he was caught—doomed. He heard bullets tearing through the fuselage behind him and the sound seemed to send him mad. Unconsciously he did the very thing he had planned to do—the unorthodox. Instead of trying to get out of that blasting stream of lead, thereby giving himself over to certain death, he savagely shoved the stick forward and tried to ram his opponent, pressing his triggers automatically as his nose came in line with the other's.

For perhaps one second the two machines faced each other thus, not fifty feet apart, their tracer making a glittering line between them. Biggles had a fleeting glimpse of the Albatros jerking desperately sideways, at the same instant something snatched at the side of his Sidcot and a hammer-like blow smashed across his face; he slipped off on to his wing and spun. He came out of the spin tearing madly at the smashed goggles which were blinding him, spun again, and then righted the machine by sheer instinct.

Half-dazed he wiped the blood from his eyes and looked around for the machine which he knew must now be coming in for the coup-de-grace. It was nowhere in sight. It was some seconds before he picked it out, half-way to the ground, spinning viciously.

Biggles leaned back in his cockpit for a moment, sick and faint from shock and reaction. When he looked down again the black-crossed machine was a flattened wreck on the ground. Gently he turned the torn and tattered Camel for home. 'That was closish,' he muttered to himself, 'closish. I shall have to be more careful. I wonder how he did that stunt? Pity Wilks wasn't watching!'

Chapter 6
Camouflage

From his elevated position in the cockpit of a Camel, Biggles surveyed the scene below him dispassionately. An intricate tracery of thin white lines marked the trench system where half a million men were locked in a life and death struggle, and a line of tiny white puffs, looking ridiculously harmless from the distance, showed the extent of the artillery barrage of flame and hurtling steel.

He turned eastward into enemy country and subjected every inch of the sky to a searching scrutiny. For a few minutes he flew thus, keeping a watchful eye upwards and occasionally glancing downwards to check his landmarks. During one of these periodical inspections of the country below something caught his eye which caused him to prolong his examination; he tilted his wing to see more clearly.

'Well, I'm dashed,' he muttered to himself; 'funny I've never noticed that before.' The object that had excited his curiosity was commonplace enough; it was simply a small church on a slight eminence. His eye followed the winding road to where it crossed the main Lille road and thence to the small hamlet of Bonvillier, which the church was evidently intended to serve. 'I could have sworn the church was in the middle of the village,' he thought. 'Dammit, it is,' he said aloud, as his eye fell on a square-towered building in the market place. 'Two churches, eh? They must have religious mania,' he mused. 'I expect the other is a chapel; funny I've never noticed it before, it's plain enough to see, in all conscience.'

He turned back towards the lines, and after another penetrating examination of the surrounding atmosphere, glanced at his map to pin-point* the chapel. It was not shown. He made a wide circle, wing down, side-slipping to lose height quickly, and, ignoring the inevitable salvo of archie, took a closer look at the building which had intrigued him. Pretty old place, he commented, as he picked out the details of ivy-covered masonry, the crumbling tombstones and the neat flower beds that bordered the curé's residence.

An exceptionally close burst of archie reminded him that he was dangerously low over the enemy lines, and as he was at the end of his patrol he dived for home, emptying his guns into the Boche support trenches as he passed over them.

Arriving back at the aerodrome, he landed and made his way slowly to the Squadron office. Colonel Raymond, of Wing Headquarters, who was in earnest conversation with Major Mullen, the C.O., broke off to nod a greeting.

'Morning, Bigglesworth,' he called cheerfully.

'Good morning, sir,' replied Biggles. 'No more packets for me to fetch, I hope,' he added with a grin.

'No,' responded the Colonel seriously, 'but I'm a bit worried all the same. We can't locate that damned heavy gun the Boche are using against our rest camps. I've had every likely area photographed, but we can't

---

* During the War maps were divided and subdivided into squares. By naming the letters and numbers of the squares, any single spot, almost to the yard, could be named and identified. This was known as pin-pointing.

find the blaze* anywhere. Haven't seen a loose gun anywhere, I suppose?'

Biggles shook his head. 'I haven't seen a damned thing the whole afternoon,' he replied bitterly, 'except a church I didn't know existed.' He took a pencil off the Major's desk and marked the position carefully on his map.

The Colonel, glancing over his shoulder, smiled with superior wisdom. 'You've got that wrong,' he said, 'there's no church there.'

Mahoney and several other officers entered the room to write their combat reports, but Biggles heeded them not.

'What do you mean, sir?' he asked, a trifle nettled. 'I know a church when I see one.'

'What sort of church is it?' asked Colonel Raymond.

Biggles described it briefly.

'Why, that's the church on the hill at Berniet,' smiled the Colonel.

'Berniet!' cried Biggles, 'but I haven't been near Berniet this morning. I beg your pardon, sir, but I saw that church here,' and he indicated the position at Bonvillier, emphatically, with the point of a pencil.

Colonel Raymond shook his head. 'Look,' he said suddenly, and selecting a photograph from a folio on the table, passed it across. 'Those photos were taken yesterday. There is Bonvillier, there are the cross-roads—there's no church, as you can see.' Biggles stared at the photographs in comical amazement, and then frowned.

---

* The line of burnt or flattened grass in front of the muzzle of a gun, caused by the flash. It showed up plainly in air photographs and betrayed many batteries.

'You're wrong, Biggles, there's no church there,' broke in Mahoney.

Biggles wheeled round in a flash. 'Are you telling me that I can't read a map, or that I don't know where I am when I'm flying?' he snapped.

'Looks like it,' grinned the other Flight-Commander, frankly, amid laughter. Biggles sprang to his feet, white with anger. 'Funny, aren't you?' he sneered; 'all right, we'll see who's right.'

He went out and slammed the door behind him.

On a dawn patrol the following morning he flew to Bonvillier, and looked down confidently for the church. His eye picked out the white ribbon of road. 'There's the crossroads—the village—well, I'm damned!' He stared as if fascinated at the spot where, the afternoon before, he thought he had located the sacred building. He pushed up his goggles and examined both sides of the road minutely, but only empty fields met his gaze. 'I'm going crazy,' he told himself bitterly, 'I'll soon be for H.E.* at this rate; I'm beginning to see things. Well, it isn't there. Let's have a look at Berniet.'

Ten minutes later he was circling high above the other village looking for the church, but in vain. 'Ha! ha!' he laughed. 'Damn good, we're all wrong; it isn't here, either.' Suddenly he became serious. 'If it isn't here, where the devil is it?' he mused. 'There must *be* a church, because the others have seen it; the thing can't walk, not complete with churchyard, ivy and gardens.' He was puzzled, and his eyes took on a thoughtful frown. 'I'll get to the bottom of this if it

* Home Establishment.

78

takes me all day,' he promised himself, and settled down for the search.

For an hour or more he flew up and down the line, systematically examining the ground section by section, and was about to abandon his self-appointed task when he came upon it suddenly, and the discovery gave him something like a shock. He was studying a wood, far over the lines, which he suspected concealed an archie battery that was worrying him, when his eyes fell on the well-remembered ivy-clad walls, crumbling tombstones and well-kept rectory gardens. It nestled snugly by the edge of the wood, half a mile from a row of tumble-down cottages.

'So there you are,' he muttered grimly. 'I'll have a closer look at you and then I'll know you next time I see you.' He shoved the stick forward and tore down in a long, screaming dive that brought him to within 1,000 feet of his objective. As he flattened out, his eyes still on the church, he caught his breath suddenly and swerved away. The Camel lurched drunkenly as a stab-bing flame split the air and a billow of black smoke blossomed out not thirty yards away. Another appeared in front of him and something smashed through his left wing not a foot from the fuselage. In a moment the air about him was full of vicious jabs of flame and swirling smoke.

'My God!' grunted Biggles, as he twisted like a wounded bird in the sea of flying steel and high explo-sive. 'What have I barged into?' He put his nose down until the needle of the speed indicator rested against the pin, and then, thirty feet from the ground, sped out of the vicinity like a startled snipe.

'Good Lord,' he said, weakly, as the fusillade died away behind him; 'What a mazurka.' He tore across the lines amid a hail of machine-gun bullets, and landing on the aerodrome ran swiftly to the Squadron office. The C.O., he was told, was in the air. He seized the telephone and called Wing Headquarters, asking for Colonel Raymond.

'I've found the church, sir,' he called as the Colonel's voice came over the 'phone.

'What about it? I'll tell you. It isn't at Berniet—I beg your pardon, sir—I didn't mean to be impertinent, but it's a fact. It isn't at Bonvillier, either. I spent the morning looking for it and finally ran it to earth on the edge of the oblong-shaped wood just east of Morslede. Funny, did you say, sir? Yes, it is funny; but I've got something still funnier to tell you. That damn tabernacle's on wheels; it moves about after dark—*and the gun you are looking for is inside it.* Just a moment, sir, I'll give you the pin-point. What's that, sir? Shoot! Good, I'll go and watch the fireworks.'

Twenty minutes later, from a safe altitude, he watched with marked approval salvo after salvo of shells, hurled by half a dozen batteries of howitzers,* tearing the surface off the earth and pounding the 'church' and its contents to mangled pulp. An R.E.8** circled above, doing the shoot***, keeping the gunners on their mark.

'That little lot should teach you to stay put in future,' commented Biggles drily, as he turned for home.

---

* A short-barrelled large-bore gun which fires a heavy shell for short-range firing.
** British two seater biplane, designed for reconnaissance and artillery observation.
*** An aircraft pin-pointing a target for the artillery below. The pilot would check how close the shells were falling to the target, then signal to the gunners below using morse code transmitted by a one-way radio.

Chapter 7
The Carrier

Biggles sat shivering in the tiny cockpit of his Camel at rather less than 1,000 feet above the Allied reserve trenches. It was a bitterly cold afternoon; the icy edge of the February wind whipped round his face and pierced the thick padding of his Sidcot suit as he tried to snuggle lower in his 'office'.

The little salient on his right was being slowly pinched out by a detachment of infantry; to Biggles it seemed immaterial whether the line was straightened out or not, a few hundred yards one way or the other was neither here nor there, he opined. He was to change his mind before the day was out. Looking down he could see the infantry struggling through the mud from shell-hole to shell-hole, as inch by inch they drove the enemy back.

Squadron orders for the day had been to help them in every possible way by strafing back areas with machine-gun fire and 20-lb. Cooper bombs to prevent the enemy from bringing up reinforcements. He had been at it all morning, and as he climbed into the cockpit for the afternoon 'show', he anticipated another miserable two hours watching mud-coated men and lumbering tanks crossing no-man's-land, as he dodged to and fro through a venomous fire from small-arms, field guns and archie batteries.

He was flying a zig-zag course behind the British lines, keeping a watchful eye open for the movements of enemy troops, although the smoke of the barrage, laid down to protect the advancing troops, made the ground difficult to see. It also served to some extent to conceal him from the enemy gunners. From time to time he darted across the line of smoke and raked the German front line with bullets from his twin Vickers guns. It was a highly dangerous, and, to Biggles, an unprofitable pursuit; he derived no sense of victory from the performance, and the increasing number of holes in his wings annoyed him intensely. 'I'll have one of those damned holes in *me* in a minute,' he grumbled.

Crash! Something had hit the machine and splashed against his face, smothering his goggles with a sticky substance. 'What the hell has happened now?' he muttered, snatching off the goggles. His first thought was that an oil lead had been cut by a piece of shell, and he instinctively throttled back and headed the Camel, nose down, farther behind his own lines.

He wiped his hand across his face and gave a cry of dismay as it came away covered in blood. 'My God! I'm hit,' he groaned, and looked anxiously below for a suitable landing ground. He had little time in which to choose, but fortunately there were many large fields handy, and a few seconds later the machine had run to a standstill in one of them.

He stood erect in the cockpit and felt himself all over, looking for the source of the gore. His eyes caught sight of a cluster of feathers stuck on the centre section bracing wires, and he sank down limply, grinning sheepishly. 'Holy mackerel,' he muttered, 'a bird! So that was it.' Closer investigation revealed more feathers, and finally he found a mangled mass of blood and feathers on the floor of the cockpit. 'The propeller must have caught it and chucked what was left of it back through the centre-section into my face,' he mused. 'Looks like a pigeon. Oh, well!—'

He made to throw it overboard, when something caught his eye. It was a tiny tube attached to the bird's leg. 'A carrier pigeon, eh?' he whistled. 'I wonder if it is one of ours or a Boche?' He knew, of course, that carrier pigeons were used extensively by both sides, but particularly by the Allies for the purpose of conveying messages from spies within the occupied territory.

Sitting on the 'hump' of his Camel he removed the capsule and extracted a small flimsy piece of paper. One glance at the jumbled lines of letters and numbers was sufficient to show him that the message was in code. 'I'd better get this to Intelligence right away,' he thought and looked up to see an officer and several Tommies regarding him curiously from the hedge.

'Are you all right?' called the officer.

'Yes,' replied Biggles. 'Do you know if there is a field telephone anywhere near?'

'There's one at Divisional Headquarters—the farmhouse at the end of the road,' was the answer.

'Can I get through to 91st Wing from there?'

'I don't know.'

'All right, many thanks,' called Biggles. 'I'll go and find out. Will you keep an eye on my machine? Thanks.'

Five minutes later he was speaking to Colonel Raymond at Wing Headquarters, and after explaining what had happened, at the Colonel's invitation, read out the message letter by letter. 'Shall I hold on?' asked Biggles at the end.

'No, ring off, but don't go away. I'll call you in a minute or two,' said the Colonel crisply.

Five minutes passed quickly as Biggles warmed himself by the office fire, and then the 'phone bell rang shrilly.

'For you, sir,' said the orderly,* handing him the instrument.

'Is that you, Bigglesworth?' came the Colonel's voice.

'Yes, sir.'

'All right, we shan't want you again.'

'Hope I brought you good news,' said Biggles, preparing to ring off.

'No, you brought bad news. The message is from one of our fellows over the other side. The machine that went to fetch him last night force-landed and killed the pilot. That's all.'

'But what about the sp—man?' asked Biggles aghast.

'I'm afraid he is in a bad case, poor devil. He says he is on the north side of Lagnicourt Wood. The Huns have got a cordon of troops all round him and are hunting him down with dogs. He's heard them.'

'My God, how awful!'

'Well, we can't help him, he knows that. It will be dark in an hour and we daren't risk a night landing without looking over the ground. They'll have got him by to-morrow. Well, thanks for the prompt way you got the message to us. By the way, your M.C.** is through; it will be in orders to-night. Good-bye.' There was a click as the Colonel rang off.

Biggles sat with the receiver in his hand. He was not thinking about the decoration the Colonel had just mentioned. He was visualizing a different scene from the one that would be enacted in mess that night when his name appeared in orders on the notice board. In

---

* Private or non-commissioned officer detailed to assist senior officers.
** Military Cross, a medal.

his mind's eye he saw a cold-bleak landscape of leafless trees through which crawled an unkempt, mud-stained, hunted figure, looking upwards to the sky for the help that would never come. He saw a posse of hard-faced grey-coated Prussians holding the straining hounds on a leash, drawing ever nearer to the fugitive. He saw a grim, blank wall against which 'stood a blindfolded man—the man who had fought the war his own way, without hope of honour, and had lost.

Biggles, after two years of war, had little of the milk of human kindness left in his being, but the scene brought a lump into his throat. 'So they'd leave him there, eh?' he thought. 'That's Intelligence, is it? No, by God,' he ground out aloud through clenched teeth, and slammed the receiver down with a crash.

'What's that, sir?' asked the startled orderly.

'Go to hell,' snapped Biggles. 'No, I didn't mean that. Sorry,' and made for the door.

He was thinking swiftly as he hurried back to the Camel. 'North edge of Lagnicourt Wood the Colonel said; it's damn nearly a mile long. I wonder if he'd spot me if I got down. He'd have to come back on the wing—it's the only way, but even that's a better chance than the firing party'll give him. We'll try it, anyway, it isn't more than seven or eight miles over the line.'

Within five minutes Biggles was in the air heading for the wood, and ten minutes later, after being badly archied, he was circling over it at 5,000 feet.

'They haven't got him yet, anyway,' he muttered, for signs of the pursuit were at once apparent. Several groups of soldiers were beating the ditches at the west end of the wood and he saw hounds working along a hedge that ran diagonally into its western end. Sentries were standing at intervals on the northern and southern sides.

'Well, there's one thing I can do in case all else fails. I'll lay my eggs first,' he decided, thinking of the two Cooper bombs that still hung on their racks. He pushed the stick forward and went tearing down at the bushes where the hounds were working.

He did a vertical turn round the bushes at fifty feet, levelled out, and, as he saw the group just over the junction of his right-hand lower plane and the fuselage, he pulled the bomb toggle, one—two. Zooming high, he half rolled, and then came down with both Vickers guns spitting viciously. A cloud of smoke prevented him from seeing how much damage had been done by the bombs. He saw a helmeted figure raise a rifle to shoot at him, fall, pick himself up, fall again, and crawl into the undergrowth. One of the hounds was dragging itself away. Biggles pulled the Camel up, turned, and came down again, his tracer making a straight line to the centre of the now clearing smoke. Out of the corner of his eye he saw other groups hurrying towards the scene, and made a mental note that he had at least drawn attention to himself, which might give the spy a chance to make a break.

He levelled out to get his bearings. Left rudder, stick over, and he was racing low over the wood towards the northern edge. At thirty feet from the ground he tore along the side of the wood, hopping the trees and hedges in his path. There was only one field large enough for him to land in; would the spy realize that, he wondered, as he swung round in a steep climbing turn and started to glide down, blipping* his engine as he came.

He knew that he was taking a desperate chance. A

* Opening and closing the throttle, to alter the sound of the engine, often used as a signal.

bad landing or a single well-aimed shot from a sentry when he was on the ground would settle the matter. His tail-skid dragged on the rough surface of the field; a dishevelled figure, crouching low, broke from the edge of the wood and ran for dear life towards him. Biggles kicked on rudder and taxied, tail up, to meet him, swinging round while still thirty yards away, ready for the take-off.

A bullet smashed through the engine cowling; another struck the machine somewhere behind him. 'Come on!' he yelled frantically, although it was obvious that the man was doing his best. 'On the wing— not that—the left one—only chance,' he snapped.

The exhausted man made no answer, but flung himself at full length on the plane, close to the fuselage, and gripped the leading edge with his bare fingers.

'Catch!' cried Biggles, and flung his gauntlets on the wing within reach of the fugitive.

Bullets were flicking up the earth about them, but they suddenly ceased, and Biggles looked up to ascertain the reason. A troop of Uhlans* were coming down the field at full gallop, not a hundred yards away. Tight-lipped, Biggles thrust the throttle open and tore across the field towards them. His thumbs sought the Bowden lever of his Vickers guns and two white pencil lines of tracer connected the muzzles with the charging horsemen.

A bullet struck a strut near his face with a crash that he could hear above the noise of his engine, and he winced. Zooming high he swung round towards the lines. 'I've got him—I've brought it off!' hammered exultantly through his brain. 'If the poor devil doesn't

* German cavalry.

87

freeze to death and fall off, I'll have him home within ten minutes.' With his altimeter needle touching 4,000 feet he pulled the throttle back and leaning out of the cockpit yelled at the top of his voice, 'Ten minutes!' A quick nod told him that the spy had understood.

Biggles pushed the stick forward and dived for the line. He could feel the effect of the drag* of the man's body, but as it counterbalanced the torque** of his engine to some extent it did not seriously interfere with the performance of the machine.

He glanced behind. A group of small black dots stood out boldly against the setting sun. Fokkers! 'You can't catch me, I'm home,' jeered Biggles, pushing the stick further forward. He was down to 2,000 feet now, his air speed indicator showing 150 m.p.h.; only another two miles now, he thought with satisfaction.

Whoof! Whoof! Whoof! Three black clouds of smoke blossomed out in front of him, and he swerved. Whoof!—Spang! Something smashed against the engine with a force that made the Camel quiver. The engine raced, vibrating wildly, and then cut out dead. For a split second Biggles was stunned. Mechanically he pushed his stick forward and looked down. The German support trenches lay below. 'My God! what luck; I can't do it,' he grated bitterly. 'I'll be three hundred yards short.' He began a slow glide towards the Allied front line, now in sight.

At 500 feet, and fast losing height, the man on the wing twisted his head round, and the expression on his face haunted Biggles for many a day. A sudden thought struck him and an icy hand clutched his heart. 'By

* Wind-resistance.
** The reaction of a propeller which tends to turn an aeroplane in the opposite direction to which the propeller is turning.

heavens! I'm carrying a professed spy; they'll shoot us both!'

The ground was very close now and he could see that he would strike it just behind the Boche front line. 'I should think the crash will kill us both,' he muttered grimly, as he eyed the sea of shell-holes below. At five feet he flattened out for pancake landing*; the machine started to sink, slowly, and then with increasing speed. A tearing, ripping crash and the Camel closed up around him; something struck him on the head and everything went dark.

'Here, take a drink of this, young feller—it's rum,' said a voice that seemed far away.

Biggles opened his eyes and looked up into the anxious face of an officer in uniform and his late passenger.

'Who are you?' he asked in a dazed voice, struggling into a sitting position and taking the proffered drink.

'Major Mackay of the Royal Scots, the fust of foot, the right of the line and the pride of the British Army,' smiled his *vis-à-vis*.

'What the hell are you doing here—where are the Huns?'

'We drove 'em out this afternoon,' said the Major, 'luckily for you.'

'Damned lucky for me,' agreed Biggles emphatically.

---

* Instead of the aircraft gliding down to land, it flops down from a height of a few feet after losing flying speed.

Chapter 8
Spads and Spandaus

Biggles looked up from his self-appointed task of filling a machine-gun belt as the distant hum of an aero engine reached his ears; an S.E.5 flying low, was making for the aerodrome. The Flight-Commander watched it fixedly, a frown deepening between his eyes. He sprang to his feet, and loose rounds of ammunition falling in all directions.

'Stand by for a crash!' he snapped at the duty ambulance driver. 'Grab a Pyrene*, everybody,' he called, 'that fellow's hit; he's going to crash!'

He caught his breath as the S.E. made a sickening flat turn, but breathed a sigh of relief as it flattened out and landed clumsily. The visiting pilot taxied to the tarmac and pushed up his goggles to disclose the pale but smiling face of Wilkinson, of 287 Squadron.

'You hit, Wilks?' called Biggles anxiously.

'No.'

Biggles grinned his relief and cast a quick, critical glance at the machine. The fabric of the wings was ripped in a dozen places; an interplane strut was shattered and the tail unit was as full of holes as the rose of a watering-can.

'Have you got a plague of rats or something over at your place?' he inquired, pointing at the holes. 'You want to get some cats.'

---

* Hand-held fire extinguisher.

'The rats that did that have red noses, and it'll take more than cats to catch 'em,' said Wilkinson meaningly, climbing stiffly out of the cockpit.

'Red noses, did you say?' said Biggles, the smile fading from his face. 'You mean—'

'The Richthofen crowd have moved down, that's what I mean,' replied Wilkinson soberly. 'I've lost Browne and Chadwicke, although I believe Browne managed to get down just over our side of the line. There must have been over twenty Huns in the bunch we ran into.'

'What were they flying?'

'Albatroses. I counted sixteen crashes on the ground between Le Cateau and here, theirs and ours. There's an R.E.8 on its nose between the lines. There's a Camel and an Albatros piled up together in the Hun front line trench. What are we going to do about it?'

'Pray for dud weather, and pray hard,' said Biggles grimly. 'See any Camels on your way?'

Wilkinson nodded. 'I saw three near Mossyface Wood.'

'That'd be Mac; he's got Batty and a new man with him.'

'Well, they'll have discovered there's a war on by now,' observed Wilkinson. 'Do you feel like making Fokker fodder of yourself, or what about running down to Clarmes for a drink and talk things over?'

'Suits me,' replied Biggles, 'I've done two patrols to-day and I'm tired. Come on; I'll ask the C.O. if we can have the tender.'

Half an hour later they pulled up in front of the Hôtel de Ville, in Clarmes. In the courtyard stood a magnificent touring car which an American staff officer had just vacated. Lost in admiration, Biggles took a step towards it.

'Thinking of buying it?' said a voice at his elbow.

Turning, Biggles beheld a Captain of the American Flying Corps. 'Why, are you thinking of selling it?' he asked evenly.

As he turned and joined Wilkinson at a table, the American seated himself near them. 'You boys just going up to the line,' he asked, 'because if you are I'll give you a tip or two.'

Biggles eyed the speaker coldly. 'Are you just going up?' he inquired.

'Sure,' replied the American, 'I'm commanding the 299th Pursuit Squadron. We moved in to-day—we shall be going over to-morrow.'

'I see,' said Biggles slowly, 'then I'll give *you* a tip. Don't cross the line under fifteen thousand.'

The American flushed. 'I wasn't asking you for advice,' he snapped; 'we can take care of ourselves.'

Biggles finished his drink and left the room.

'That baby fancies himself a bit,' observed the American to Wilkinson. 'When he's heard a gun or two go off he won't be so anxious to hand out advice. Who is he?'

'His name's Bigglesworth,' said Wilkinson civilly. 'Officially, he's only shot down twelve Huns and five balloons, but to my certain knowledge he's got several more.'

'That kid? Say, don't try that on me, brother. You've got a dozen Huns, too, I expect,' jibed the American.

'Eighteen, to be precise,' said Wilkinson, casually tapping a cigarette.

The American paused with his drink half-way to his

lips. He set the glass back on the table. 'Say, do you mean that?' he asked incredulously.

Wilkinson shrugged his shoulders, but did not reply.

'What did he mean when he said not to cross the line under fifteen thousand?' asked the American curiously.

'I think he was going to tell you that the Richthofen circus had just moved in opposite,' explained Wilkinson.

'I've heard of that lot,' admitted the American, 'who are they?'

Wilkinson looked at him in surprise. 'They are a big bunch of star pilots, each with a string of victories to his credit. They hunt together, and are led by Manfred Richthofen, whose score stands at about seventy. With him he's got his brother, Lothar—with about thirty victories. There's Gussmann and Wolff and Weiss, all old hands at the game. There's Karjus, who has only one arm, but shoots better than most men with two. Then there's Lowenhardt, Reinhard, Udet and—but what does it matter? A man who hasn't been over the line before, meeting that bunch, has about as much chance as a rabbit in a wild beast show,' he concluded.

'You trying to put the wind up me?'

'No. I'm just telling you why Biggles said don't cross under 15,000 feet. You may then have a chance to dive home if you meet 'em. That's all. Well, cheerio, see you later perhaps.'

'It's a damn shame,' raved Biggles, as they drove back to the aerodrome. 'Some of these Americans are the best stuff in the world. One of two of 'em have been out here for months with our own squadrons and the French Lafayette and Cigognes Escadrilles.* Now their

* French fighter and bomber squadrons.

brass-hats have pulled 'em out and rolled 'em into their own Pursuit Squadrons. Do they put them in charge because they know the game? Do they—Hell! No. They hand 'em over to some poor boob who has done ten hours solo in Texas or somewhere, but has got a command because his sister's in the Follies; and they've got to follow where he leads 'em. Bah! It makes me sick. You heard that poor prune just now? He'll go beetling over at five thousand just to show he knows more about it than we do. Well, he'll be pushing up the Flanders poppies by this time to-morrow night unless a miracle happens. He'll take his boys with him, that's the curse of it. Not one of 'em'll ever get back—you watch it,' he concluded, bitterly.

'We can't let 'em do that,' protested Wilkinson.

'What can we do?'

'I was just thinking.'

'I've got it,' cried Biggles. 'Let them be the bait to bring the Huns down. With your S.E.'s and our Camels together, we'll knock the spots off that Hun circus. How many S.E.'s can you raise?'

'Eight or nine.'

'Right. You ask your C.O. and let me know to-night. I'll ask Major Mullen for all the Camels we can get in the air. That should even things up a bit; we'll be strong enough to take on anything the Huns can send against us. I'll meet you over Mossyface at six. How's that?'

'Suits me. I hope it's a fine day,' yawned Wilkinson.

The show turned out to be a bigger one than Biggles anticipated. Major Mullen had decided to lead the entire Squadron himself, not so much on account of the possibility of the American Squadron being massacred, as because he realized the necessity of massing his machines to meet the new menace.

Thus it came about that the morning following his conversation with Wilkinson found Biggles leading his flight behind the C.O. On his right was 'A' Flight, led by Mahoney, and on his left 'B' Flight, with MacLaren at their head. Each Flight comprised three machines, and these, with Major Mullen's red-cowled Camel, made ten in all. Major Sharp, commanding the S.E.5 Squadron, had followed Major Mullen's example, and from time to time Biggles looked upwards and backwards to where a formation of nine tiny dots, 6,000 feet above them, showed where the S.E.'s were watching and waiting. A concerted plan of action had been decided upon, and Biggles impatiently awaited its consummation.

Where were the Americans? He asked himself the question for the tenth time; they were a long time showing up. Where was the Boche circus? Sooner or later there was bound to be a clash, and Biggles thrilled at the thought of the coming dog-fight.

It was a glorious day; not a cloud broke the serenity of the summer sky. Biggles kept his eyes downwards, knowing that the S.E.'s would prevent molestation from above. Suddenly, a row of minute moving objects caught his eye, and Biggles stared in amazement. Then he swore. A formation of nine Spads* was crossing the line far below. 'The fools, the unutterable lunatics,' he growled, 'they can't be an inch higher than four thousand. They must think they own the sky, and they

* A French-made fighting biplane Scout which first appeared in 1916, top speed 132 m.p.h. armed with one or two Vickers machine guns. It was used by the US when they formed their own squadrons.

haven't even seen us yet. Oh, well, they'll wake up presently, or I'm no judge.'

The Spad Squadron was heading out straight into enemy sky, and Biggles watched them with amused curiosity, uncertain as to whether to admire their nerve or curse their stupidity. 'They must think it's easy,' he commented grimly, as his lynx-eyed leader altered his course slightly to follow the Americans.

Where were the Huns? He held his hand, at arm's length, over the sun, and extending his fingers squinted through the slits between them. He could see nothing, but the glare was terrific and might have concealed a hundred machines.

'They're there, I'll bet my boots,' muttered the Flight-Commander; 'they are just letting those poor boobs wade right into the custard. How they must be laughing!'

Suddenly he stiffened in his seat. The Major was rocking his wings—pointing. Biggles followed the out-stretched finger and caught his breath. Six brightly painted machines were going down in an almost verti-cal dive behind the Spads. Albatroses. He lifted his hand high above his head, and then, in accordance with the plan, pushed the stick forward and, with Batson and Healy on either side, tore down diagonally to cut off the enemy planes. He knew that most of the Hun circus was still above, somewhere, waiting for the right moment to come down. How long would they wait before coming down, thus bringing the rest of the Camels and S.E.'s down into the mix-up with them? Not long he hoped, or he might find his hands full, for he could not count upon the inexperienced Spad pilots for help.

The Spad Squadron had not altered its course, and

Biggles' lip curled as he realized that even now they had not seen the storm brewing above them. Ah! they knew now. The Albatroses were shooting, and the Spads swerved violently, like a school of minnows at the sudden presence of a pike. In a moment all formation was lost as they scattered in all directions. Biggles sucked in his breath quickly as a Spad burst into flames and dropped like a stone. He was among them now; a red-bellied machine appeared through his sights and he pressed his triggers viciously, cursing a Spad that nearly collided with him.

A green Albatros came at him head-on, and as he charged it, another, with a blue and white checked fuselage sent a stream of tracer through his top plane. The green machine swerved and he flung the Camel round behind it; but the checked machine had followed him and he had to pull up in a wild zoom to escape the hail of lead it spat at him. 'Hell!' grunted Biggles vigorously, as his wind-screen flew to pieces, 'this is getting too hot. My God, what a mess!' A Spad and an Albatros, locked together, careered earthwards in a flat spin. A Camel, spinning viciously, whirled past him, and another Albatros, wrapped in a sheet of flame, flashed past his nose, the doomed pilot leaping into space even as it passed.*

Biggles snatched a swift glance upwards. A swarm of Albatroses were dropping like vultures out of the sky into the fight; he had a fleeting glimpse of other machines far above and then he turned again to the work on hand. Where were the Spads? Ah, there was one, on the tail of an Albatros. He tore after it, but the Spad pilot saw him and waved him away. Biggles

* Very few pilots carried parachutes during the First World War so to leap from a plane meant certain death.

grinned. 'Go to it, laddie,' he yelled exultantly, but a frown swept the grin from his face as a jazzed machine darted in behind the Spad and poured in a murderous stream of lead. Biggles shot down on the tail of the Hun. The Spad pilot saw the danger and twisted sideways to escape, but an invisible cord seemed to hold the Albatros to the tail of the American machine. Biggles took the jazzed machine in his sights and raked it from end to end in a long deadly burst. There was no question of missing at that range; the enemy pilot slumped forward in his seat and the machine went to pieces in the air.

The Spad suddenly stood up on its tail and sent two white pencils of tracer across Biggle's nose at something he could not see. A Hun, upside down, went past him so closely that he instinctively flinched. 'My God!' muttered Biggles, 'he saved *me* that time; that evens things up.'

His lips closed in a straight line; a bunch of six Albatroses were coming at him together. Biggles fired one shot, and went as cold as ice as his gun jammed. Bullets were smashing through his machine when a cloud of S.E.'s appeared between him and the Hun, and he breathed again. 'Lord, what a dog-fight,' he said again, as he looked around to see what was happening. Most of the enemy planes were in full retreat, pursued by the S.E.'s. Two Camels and two Albatroses were still circling some distance away and four more Camels were rallying above him. Biggles saw the lone Spad flying close to him. Seven or eight crashed machines were on the ground, two blazing furiously, but whether they were Spads or Camels he couldn't tell.

He pushed up his goggles and beckoned to the Spad

pilot, whom he now recognized as his acquaintance of the previous day, to come closer.

The American waved gaily, and together they started after the Camels, led by Major Mullen's red cowling, now heading for the line . . . Biggles landed with the Spad still beside him; he mopped the burnt castor oil off his face and walked across to meet the pilot. The American held out his hand. 'I just dropped in to shake hands,' he said. 'Now I must be getting back to our field to see how many of the outfit got home. I'd like to know you better; maybe you'll give me a tip or two.'

'I can't tell you much after what you've seen to-day,' laughed Biggles, turning to wave to an S.E.5, which had swung low over them and then proceeded on its way.

'Who's that?' asked the American.

'That's Wilks, the big stiff you saw with me yesterday,' replied Biggles. 'He's a good scout. He'll be at the Hôtel de Ville to-night for certain; so shall I. Do you feel like coming along to tear a chop and knock a bottle or two back?'

'Sure,' agreed the Spad pilot enthusiastically.

Chapter 9
The Zone Call

Oh, my batman awoke me from my bed,
I'd had a thick night and I'd got a sore head;
  So I said to myself,
  To myself, I said,
Oh, I haven't got a hope in the mo—orning.

So I went to the sheds to examine my gun.
And then my engine I tried to run,
  But the revs she ga-ve
  Were a thousand and one.
So I hadn't got a hope in the mo—orning.

The words of the old R.A.F. song, roared by forty youthful voices to the tune of 'John Peel', drowned the accompaniment of the cracked mess piano in spite of the strenuous efforts of the pianist to make his notes audible.

Biggles pushed the hair off his forehead. 'Lord, it's hot in here; I'm going outside for a breath of air,' he said to Wilkinson of 287 Squadron, who had come over for the periodical binge.

The two officers rose and strolled slowly towards the door. It was still daylight, but a thick layer of thundercloud hung low in the sky, making the atmosphere oppressive.

Oh, we were escorting 'twenty-two,'
Hadn't got a notion what to do,
  So, we shot down a Spa-a-d,

> And an F.E. too,
> For we hadn't—

'Stop!' Biggles had bounded back into the centre of the room and held up his arms for silence. 'Hark!' At the expression in his face a sudden hush fell upon the assembly and the next instant forty officers had stiffened into attitudes of tense expectancy as a low vibrating hum filled the air. It was the unmistakable 'pour-vous, pour-vous' of a Mercédès aero-engine, low down, not far away.

'A Hun!' The silence was broken by a wild yell and the crash of fallen chairs as Biggles darted through the open door and streaked like a madman for the sheds, shouting orders as he went. The ack-emmas had needed no warning, a Camel was already on the tarmac; others were being wheeled out with feverish speed. Capless and goggleless, tunic still thrown open at the throat, Biggles made a flying leap into the cockpit of the first Camel, and within a minute, in spite of Wilkinson's plaintive 'Wait for me,' was tearing down-wind across the sun-baked aerodrome in a cloud of dust.

He was in the air, climbing back up over the sheds, before the second machine was ready to take off. The clouds were low, and at 1,000 feet the grey mist was swirling in his slipstream. He could no longer hear the enemy plane for the roar of his Bentley Rotary drowned all other sound. He pushed his joystick forward for a moment to gather speed and then pulled it back in a swift zoom. Bursting into the sunlight above he literally flung the machine round in a lightning right-hand turn to avoid crashing into a Pfalz scout,* painted vivid scarlet with white stripes behind the pilot's seat.

---

* Very successful German single-seater biplane fighter, fitted with two or three machine guns synchronised to fire through the propeller.

'My God!' muttered Biggles, startled. 'I nearly rammed him.' He was round in a second, warming his guns as he came. The Pfalz had turned too and was now circling erratically in a desperate effort to avoid the glittering pencil lines of tracer that started at the muzzles of Biggles' guns and ended at the tail of the Boche machine. The German pilot made no attempt to retaliate, but concentrated on dodging the hail of lead, waving his left arm above his head. Biggles ceased firing and looked about him suspiciously, but not another enemy machine was in sight.

'Come on, let's get it over,' he muttered, as he thumbed his triggers again, but the Boche put his nose down and dived through the cloud, Biggles close behind him.

They emerged below the cloud bank in the same relative positions, and it at once became obvious that the German intended to land on the aerodrome, but a brisk burst of machine-gun fire from Lewis guns in front of the mess caused him to change his mind; instead, he hopped over the hedge and made a clumsy landing in the next field. Biggles landed close behind him and ran towards the pilot, now struggling to get a box of matches from his inside pocket to fire the machine.

Biggles seized him by the collar and threw him clear.

'Speak English?' he snapped.

'Yes.'

'What's the matter with you? Haven't you got any guns?' sneered the British pilot, noting the German's pale face.

'Nein, no guns,' said the German quickly.

'What?'

The German shrugged his shoulders and pointed. A

swift glance showed Biggles that such was indeed the case.

'My God!' he cried aghast. 'You people running short of weapons or something? We'd better lend you some.'

'I vas lost,' said the German pilot resignedly. 'I am to take a new Pfalz to Lille, but the clouds—I cannot see. The benzine is nearly finished. You come—I come down, so.'

'Tough luck,' admitted Biggles as a crowd of officers and ack-emmas arrived on the scene at the double. 'Well, come and have a drink—you've butted into a party.'

'Huh! no wonder your crowd score if you go about shooting at delivery pilots,' grinned Wilkinson, who had just landed.

'You go and stick your face in an oil sump, Wilks,' cried Biggles hotly. 'How did I know he hadn't any guns?'

Biggles sprang lightly from the squadron tender and looked at the deserted aerodrome in astonishment. It was the morning following his encounter with the unarmed Pfalz. For some days a tooth had been troubling him, and on the advice of the Medical Officer he had been to Clarmes to have the offending molar extracted. He had not hurried back, as the M.O. had forbidden him to fly that day, and now he had returned to find every machine except his own in the air.

'Where have they all gone, Flight?' he asked the Flight-Sergeant.

'Dunno, sir. The C.O. came out in a hurry about an hour ago and they all went off together,' replied the N.C.O.

'Just my luck,' grumbled Biggles, 'trust something to happen when I'm away for a few hours! Oh, well!'

He made his way to the Squadron Office where he found Tyler, commonly know as 'Wat,' the Recording Officer,* busy with some papers.

'What's on, Wat?' asked Biggles.

'Escort.'

'Escorting what?'

'You remember that Hun you got yesterday?'

Biggles nodded.

'Well, apparently he was three sheets in the wind when Wing came and fetched him. He blabbed a whole lot of news to the Intelligence people. This is what he told 'em. He said that three new Staffels were being formed at Lagnicourt. A whole lot of new machines were being sent there; in fact, when he was there two days ago, over thirty machines were being assembled.'

'Funny, him letting a thing like that drop,' interrupted Biggles. 'He didn't strike me as being blotto, either. He drank practically nothing.'

'Well, Wing says he was as tight as a lord, and bragged that the three new circuses were going to wipe us off the map, so they decided to nip the plot in the bud. They've sent every machine they can get into the air with a full load of bombs to fan the whole caboodle sky-high—all the Fours, Nines, and Biffs** have gone, and even the R.E.8's they can spare from Art. Obs.*** Two-eight-seven, two-nine-nine and our people are escorting 'em.'

'Well, they can have it,' said Biggles cheerfully. 'Escorting's a mouldy business, anyway. Thanks, Wat.'

* The officer designated to supervise all the Squadron records.
** Slang: Bristol Fighters.
*** Artillery observation.

He strolled out on to the aerodrome, gently rubbing his lacerated jaw, and catching sight of the German machine now standing on the tarmac, made his way slowly towards it. He examined it with interest, for a complete ready-to-fly-away Boche machine was a *rara avis*. He slipped his hand into the map case, but the maps had been removed. His fingers felt and closed around a torn piece of paper at the bottom of the lining; it was creased as if had been roughly torn off and used to mark a fold in a map. Biggles glanced at it disinterestedly, noting some typewritten matter on it, but as it was in German and conveyed nothing to him he was about to throw it away when the Flight-Sergeant passed near him.

'Do you speak German, Flight?' called Biggles.

'No, sir, but Thompson does; he used to be in the Customs office or something like that,' replied the N.C.O.

'Ask him to come here a minute, will you?' said Biggles.

'Can you tell me what that says?' he asked a moment later, as an ack-emma approached him and saluted.

The airman took the paper and looked at it for a minute without speaking. 'It's an extract from some orders, sir,' he said at length. 'The first part of it's gone, but this is what it says, roughly speaking: "With effect"—there's a bit gone there—"any flieger"—flyer, that is—"falling into the hands of the enemy will therefore repeat that three Jagdstaffels are being assembled at Langi—" can't read the place, sir. "By doing so, he will be doing service by assisting"—can't read that, sir. It ends, "Expires on July 21st at twelve, midnight. This order must on no account be taken into the air." That's all, sir.'

'Read that again,' said Biggles slowly.

After the airman had obeyed Biggles returned to the Squadron office deep in thought. He put a call through to Wing Headquarters and asked for Colonel Raymond.

'That you, sir? Bigglesworth here,' he said, as the Colonel's crisp voice answered him. 'About this big raid, sir. Do you mind if I ask whether you know for certain that these Boche machines are at Lagnicourt?'

'Yes, we made reconnaisance at dawn, and the observer reported several machines in various stages of erection on the tarmac. Why do you ask?'

'I've just found a bit of paper in the Pfalz the Boche brought over. I can't read it because it's in German, but I've had it translated, and it looks as if that Hun had orders to tell you that tale. Will you send over for it?'

'I'll send a messenger for it right away, but I shouldn't worry about it; the Huns are there, we've seen them. Good-bye.'

Biggles hung the receiver up slowly and turned to Wat, who had listened to the conversation.

'You'll get shot one day ringing up the Wing like that!' he said reprovingly.

'It would be a hell of a joke to send forty machines to drop twenty thousand quid's worth of bombs on a lot of obsolete spare parts,' mused Biggles; 'but there's more in it than that. The Boche want our machines out of the way. Why? That's what I want to know. Lagnicourt lies thirty miles north-west of here. I fancy it wouldn't be a bad idea if somebody went and had a dekko what the Huns were doing in the north-east. Even my gross intelligence tells me that when a Hun is told what he's got to say when he's shot down, there's something fishy about it.'

'The M.O. says you're not to fly to-day,' protested the R.O.

'Rot! What the hell does he think I fly with, my teeth?' asked Biggles sarcastically. 'See you later.'

Within ten minutes Biggles was in the air, heading into the blue roughly to the north-east of the aerodrome. An unusual amount of archie marked his progress and he noticed it with satisfaction, for it tended to confirm his suspicions. 'What ho,' he addressed the invisible gunner, 'so you don't want any Peeping-Toms about to-day, eh? Want to discourage me.' The archie became really hot, and twice he had to circle to spoil the gunner's aim. He kept a watchful eye on the ground below, but saw nothing unusual.

He passed over an R.E.9 spotting for the artillery, manfully plodding its monotonous figure-of-eight 3,000 feet below, and nodded sympathetically. Presently he altered his course a little westerly and the archie faded away. 'Don't mind me going that way, eh? Well, let's try the other way again,' he muttered. Instantly the air was thick with black, oily bursts of smoke, and Biggles nodded understandingly. 'So I'm getting warm, am I?' he mused. 'They might as well say so; what imaginations they've got.'

Straight ahead of him, lying like a great dark green stain across the landscape, lay the forest of Duvigny. Keeping a watchful eye above for enemy aircraft, Biggles looked at it closely, but there was no sign of anything unusual about its appearance. 'I wonder if that's it?' he mused, deep in thought. 'I could soon find out; it's risky, but it's the only way.' He knew what all old pilots knew, a trick the German pilots had learned early in the War, when vast numbers of Russian troops were concealed in forests along the north-German frontier, and that was, that if an enemy plane flew low enough, the troops, no matter how well hidden, would reveal their presence by shooting at it. Not even strict orders could prevent troops from firing at an enemy aeroplane within range.

He pushed his stick forward and went roaring down at the forest. At 1,000 feet he started pulling out, but not before he had seen several hundred twinkling fireflies amongst the greenery. The fireflies were, of course, the flashes of rifles aimed at him. In one place a number of men had run out into a clearing and started firing, but an officer had driven them back. 'So that's it, is it?' muttered Biggles, thrilling with excitement. 'I wonder how many of them there are.'

Time and time again he dived low over different parts of the forest and each time the twinkling flashes betrayed the hidden troops. His wings were holed in many places, but he heeded them not. It would take a lucky shot from a rifle to bring him down. 'My God!' he muttered, as he pulled up at the far end of the forest, after his tenth dive, 'the wood's full of 'em. There must be fifty thousand men lying in that timber, and it's close to the line. They're massing for a big attack. What did those orders say? July 21st? Great God, that's to-morrow. They'll attack this afternoon, or at latest to-night. I'd better be getting out of this. So that's why they didn't want any of our machines prowling about.'

He made for the line, toying with the fine adjustment to get the very last rev. out of his engine. He could see the R.E.8 still tapping out its 'G.G.' (fire) signal to the gunners and marking the position of the falling shells, and the sight of it gave him an idea. The R.E.8 was fitted with wireless; he was not. If only he could get the pilot to send out a zone call on that wood, his work was done.*

Biggles flew close to the R.E.8, signalling to attract attention. How could he tell them, that was the problem. He flew closer and gesticulated wildly, jabbing downwards towards the wood, and then tapping with his finger on an invisible key. The pilot and observer eyed him stupidly and Biggles shrugged his shoulders in despair. Then inspiration struck him. He knew the morse code, of course, for every pilot had to pass a test in it before going to France. He flew close beside the R.E.8, raised his arm above his head and, with some difficulty, sent a series of dots and dashes. He saw the observer nod understandingly and grab a notebook to take down the message. Biggles started his signal. Dash, dash, dot dot—Z, dash, dash, dash—O, dash, dot—N, dot—E. He continued the performance until he had sent the words, 'Zone Call, Wood,' and then stabbed viciously at the wood with his forefinger. He saw the observer lean forward and have a quick,

* A Zone Call was a special call from an aircraft to the artillery and was only used in very exceptional circumstances. When the zone call was tapped out by the wireless operator it was followed by the pin-point of the target. Military maps were divided into squares and smaller squares, each square numbered and lettered. By this means it was possible to name any spot on the map instantly. When a zone call was sent out, every weapon of every calibre within range directed rapid fire on the spot, and this may have meant that hundreds of guns opened up at once on the same spot. The result can be better imagined than described. Obviously such treatment was terribly expensive, costing possibly £10,000 a minute while it lasted, and only exceptional circumstances, such as a long line of transport, or a large body of troops, warranted the call. There was a story in France of a new officer who, in desperation, sent out a zone call on a single archie battery that was worrying him. He was court-martialled and sent home.

difficult conversation with the pilot, who nodded. The observer raised both thumbs in the air and bent over his buzzer. Biggles turned away to watch the result.

Within a minute he saw the first shell explode in the centre of the wood. Another followed it, then another and another. In five minutes the place was an inferno of fire, smoke, flying timber and hurtling steel, and thousands of figures, clad in the field-grey of the German infantry, were swarming out into the open to escape the pulverizing bombardment. He could see the officers attempting to get the men into some sort of order, but there was no stemming that wild panic. They poured into the communication trenches, and others, unable to find cover, were flinging away their equipment and running for their lives.

'Holy mackerel, what a sight!' murmured Biggles. 'What a pity the Colonel isn't here to see it.' A Bristol Fighter appeared in the sky above him, heading for the scene of carnage. The observer was leaning over the side and the pilot's arm was steadily moving up and down as he exposed plate after plate in his camera. 'He'll have to believe me when he sees those photographs though,' thought Biggles.

'Well, I should think I've saved our chaps in the line a lot of trouble,' he soliloquised, as he turned to congratulate the R.E.8 crew, but the machine was far away. Biggles' Camel suddenly rocked violently and he realized the reason for the R.E.8's swift departure. He was right in the line of fire of the artillery and the shells were passing near him. He put his nose down in a fright and sped towards home in the wake of the R.E.8.

He landed on the aerodrome to find the escorting

Camels had returned, and the pilots greeted him noisily.

'Had a nice trip, chaps?' inquired Biggles.

'No,' growled Mahoney, 'didn't see a Hun the whole way out and home. These escorts bore me stiff. What have you been doing?'

'Oh, having a little fun and games on my own.'

'Who with?'

'With the German army,' said Biggles lightly.

Chapter 10
The Decoy

Biggles landed and taxied quickly up to the sheds. 'Are Mr Batson and Mr Healy home yet?' he asked the Flight-Sergeant, as he climbed stiffly from the cockpit. 'We got split up among the clouds near Ariet after a dog-fight with a bunch of Albatros.'

'Mr Healy came in about five minutes ago, sir; he's just gone along to the mess, but I haven't seen anything of Mr Batson,' replied the N.C.O.

Biggles lit a cigarette and eyed the eastern sky anxiously. He was annoyed that his flight had been broken up, although after a dog-fight it was no uncommon occurrence for machines to come home independently. He breathed a sigh of relief as the musical hum of a Bentley Rotary reached his ears, and started to walk slowly towards the mess, glancing from time to time over his shoulder at the now rapidly-approaching Camel. Suddenly he paused in his stride and looked at the wind-stocking. 'What's the young fool doing, trying to land cross-wind,' he growled, and turned round to watch the landing.

The Camel had flattened out rather too high for a good landing, and dropped quickly as it lost flying speed. The machine bumped—bumped again as the wheels bounced, and then swung round in a wide semi-circle as it ran to a standstill not fifty yards away.

Biggles opened his mouth to shout a caustic remark at the pilot, but his teeth suddenly closed with a snap, and the next instant he was running wildly towards the machine, followed by the Flight-Sergeant and several ack-emmas. He reached the Camel first, and, foot in the stirrup, swung himself up to the cockpit; one glance, and he was astride the fuselage unbuckling the safety belt around the limp figure in the pilot's seat.

'Gently, Flight-Sergeant, gently,' he said softly, as they lifted the stricken pilot from his seat and laid him carefully on the grass. Biggles caught his breath as he saw an ugly red stain on his hand that had supported the wounded pilot's back. 'How did they get you, kid?' he choked, dropping on to his knees and bending close over the ashen face.

'I—got—the—bus—home—Biggles,' whispered Batson eagerly.

'Sure you did,' nodded Biggles, fighting back a sob and forcing a smile. 'What was it, laddie—archie?'

The pilot looked at his Flight-Commander with wide open eyes. 'My own fault,' he whispered faintly . . . 'I went down—after Rumpler—with green—tail. Thought I'd—be—clever.' He smiled wanly. 'Albatroses—waiting—upstairs. It was—trap. They got me—Biggles. I'm going—topsides.'

'Not you,' said Biggles firmly, waving away Batson's mechanic who was muttering incoherently.

'It's getting dark early; where are you—Biggles—I can't see you,' went on the wounded man, his hand groping blindly for the other pilot.

'I'm here, old boy. I'm with you, don't worry,' crooned Biggles like a mother to an ailing child.

'Not worrying. Get that—Rumpler—for me—Biggles.'

'I'll get him, Batty, I'll get the swine, never fear,' replied Biggles, his lips trembling.

For a minute there was silence, broken only by the sound of a man sobbing in the distance. The wounded pilot opened his eyes, already glazed by the film of death.

'It's getting—devilish—dark—Biggles,' he whispered faintly, 'dev—lish—da—ark—'

The M.O. arrived at the double and lifted Biggles slowly, but firmly to his feet. 'Run along now, old man,' he said kindly after a swift glance at the man on the ground. 'The boy's gone.'

For a moment longer Biggles stood looking down through a mist of tears at the face of the man who had been tied to him by such bonds of friendship as only war can tie.

'I'll get him for you, Batty,' he said through his teeth, and turning, walked slowly towards the sheds.

The Rumpler with the green tail was an old menace in the sky well known to Biggles. Of a slow, obsolescent type, it looked 'easy meat' to the beginner, unaware of its sinister purpose, which was to act as a tempting bait to lure just such pilots beneath the waiting Spandau guns of the shark-like Albatroses. Once, many months before, Biggles had nearly fallen into the trap. He was going down on to an old German two-seater when a premonition of danger made him glance back over his shoulder, and the sight that greeted his eyes sent him streaking for his own side of the line as if a host of devils were on his tail—as indeed, they were.

Such death-traps were fairly common, but they no longer deceived him for an instant. 'Never go down after a Hun,' was the warning dinned into the ears of every new arrival in France by those who knew the pitfalls that awaited the unwary—alas, how often in vain.

So the old pilots, who had bought their experience, went on, and watched the younger ones come and go, unless, like Biggles, they were fortunate enough to escape, in which case the lesson was seldom forgotten.

And now the green-tailed Rumpler had killed Batty, or had led him to his doom—at least, that was what it amounted to; so reasoned Biggles. That Batson had been deceived by the trap he did not for one moment believe. The lad—to use his own words—'tried to be clever,' and in attempting to destroy the decoy, had failed, where failure could have only tragic results; and this was the machine that Biggles had pledged himself to destroy.

He had no delusions as to the dangers of the task he had undertaken. Batson's disastrous effort was sufficient proof of that. First, he must find the decoy; that should not be difficult. Above it, biding their time, would be the school of Albatroses, eyes glued downwards, waiting for the victim to walk into the trap.

Biggles sat alone in a corner of 'C' Flight hangar and wrestled with the problem, unconscious of the anxious glances and whispered consultations of his mechanics. The death of Batson had shaken him badly, and he was sick; sick of the war, sick of flying, sick of life itself. What did it matter, anyway? he mused. His turn would come, sooner or later, that was certain. He didn't attempt to deceive himself on that point. He made up his mind suddenly and called the Flight-Sergeant to him in tones that brooked no delay.

'Let's go and look at Mr Batson's machine,' he said tersely.

'I have examined it, sir,' said the N.C.O. quickly.

'It's still O.K. Hardly touched; just one burst, through back of the fuselage, down through pilot's seat and through the floor.'

'Good. I'll take it,' said Biggles coldly. 'Come and give me a swing.'

'But you're not going to—not going—'

'Do what you're told,' snapped Biggles icily. 'I'm flying that machine from now on—until—' Biggles looked the Flight-Sergeant in the eyes—'until—well—you know—' he concluded.

The N.C.O. nodded. 'Very good, sir,' he said briskly.

Five minutes later Biggles took off in the dead pilot's Camel; the Flight-Sergeant and a silent group of ack-emmas watched his departure. 'Mad as a bleedin' 'atter. Gawd 'elp the 'Un as gets in 'is way to-day,' observed a tousle-headed cockney fitter.

'Get to hell back to your work,' roared the Flight-Sergeant. 'What are you all gaping at?'

Major Mullen hurried along the tarmac. 'Who's just taken off in that machine, Flight-Sergeant?' he asked curtly.

'Mr Bigglesworth, sir.'

The C.O. gazed after the rapidly-disappearing Camel sadly. 'I see,' he said slowly, and then again, 'I see.'

The finding of the green-tailed Rumpler proved a longer job than Biggles anticipated. At the end of a week he was still searching, still flying Batson's machine, and every pilot within fifty miles knew of his quest. Major Mullen had protested; in fact, he had done everything except definitely order Biggles out of the machine; but, being a wise man and observing the high pressure under which his pilot was living, he

116

refrained from giving an order that he knew would be broken. So Biggles continued his search unhindered.

The Rumpler had become an obsession with him. For eight hours a day he hunted the sky between Lille and Cambrai for it, and at night, in his sleep, he shot it down in flames a hundred times. He had become morose, and hardly even spoke to Mac or Mahoney, the other Flight-Commanders, who watched him anxiously and secretly helped him in his search. He was due for leave, but refused to accept it. He fought many battles and, although he hardly bothered to confirm his victories, his score mounted rapidly. His combat reports were brief and contained nothing but the barest facts.

No man could stand such a pace for long. The M.O. knew it, but did nothing, although he hoped and prayed that the pilot might find his quarry before his nerves collapsed like a pack of cards.

One morning Biggles had just refuelled after a two-hour patrol and was warming up his engine again, when a D.H.9 landed, and the observer hurried towards the sheds. Dispassionately, Biggles saw him speak to the Flight-Sergeant and the N.C.O. point in his direction. The observer turned and crossed quickly to the Camel.

'Are you Bigglesworth?' he shouted above the noise of the engine.

Biggles nodded.

'I hear you're looking for that green-tailed Rumpler?'

Biggles nodded again eagerly.

'I saw it ten minutes ago, near Talcourt-le-Château.'

'Thanks,' said Biggles briefly, and pushed the throttle open.

He saw the Rumpler before he reached the lines, at least he saw the wide circles of white archie bursts that followed its wandering course. The British archie was white, and German archie black, so he knew that the plane was a German and from its locality suspected it to be the Rumpler. A closer inspection showed him that his supposition was correct. It was just over its own side of the lines, at about 8,000 feet, ostensibly engaged on artillery observation. Biggles edged away and studied the sky above it closely, but he could see nothing. He climbed steadily, keeping the Boche machine in sight, but making no attempt to approach it, and looked upwards again for the escorting Albatroses which he knew were there, but he was still unable to discover them.

'If I didn't know for certain that they were there, I should say there wasn't a Hun in the sky,' he muttered, as he headed south-east, keeping parallel with the trenches. With his eye still on the Rumpler he could have named the very moment when the Boche observer spotted him, for the machine suddenly began to edge towards him as though unaware of his presence, and seemingly unconsciously making of itself an ideal subject for attack by a scout pilot.

To an old hand like Biggles the invitation was too obvious, and even without his knowledge of the trap the action would have made him suspiciously alert. Unless he was the world's worst observer, the man in the back seat of the black-crossed machine could not have failed to have seen him, in which case he should have lost no time in placing as great a distance as possible between himself and a dangerous adversary, for the first duty of a two-seater pilot was to do his job and get home, leaving the fighting to machines designed for the purpose. Yet here was an old and comparatively unmanœuvrable machine deliberately

118

asking for trouble. 'Bah!' sneered Biggles, peeved to think he had been taken for a fool. ' "Will you step into my parlour?" said the spider to the fly. Yes, you hound, I will, but it won't be through the front door.' He looked upwards above the Rumpler, but the sun was in his eyes, so he held on his way, still climbing, and had soon left the Boche machine far below and behind him.

At 15,000 feet Biggles started to head into enemy sky, placing himself between the sun and the Rumpler, now a speck in the far distance. His roving eyes suddenly focused on a spot high over the enemy plane. 'So there you are,' he muttered grimly, 'how many?— One—two—three'—he shifted his gaze still higher— 'four—five—six—seven. Seven, in two layers, eh? Ought to be enough for a solitary Camel. Well, we'll see.'

He estimated the lowest Albatroses to be at about his own height. The other four were a couple of thousand feet higher. With the disposition of the trap now apparent he proceeded in accordance with the line of action upon which he had decided. He had already placed himself 'in the sun,' and in that position it was unlikely that he would be seen by any of the enemy pilots. He continued to climb until he was above the highest enemy formation, and then cautiously began to edge towards them, turning when they turned, and keeping in a direct line with the the sun.

He felt fairly certain that the crew of the Rumpler would ignore the possibility of danger from above on account of the escorting Albatroses, and the pilots of the enemy scouts would have their eyes on the machine below. Upon these factors Biggles planned his attack. If he was able to approach unseen he would be able to make one lightning attack almost before the Huns were aware of his presence. If he was seen, his superior altitude should give him enough extra speed to reach the lines before he was caught.

He knew he would only have time for one burst at the Rumpler. If he missed there could be no question of staying for a second attempt, for the Albatroses would be down on him like a pack of ravening wolves. The Rumpler was now flying almost directly over no-man's-land, and Biggles edged nearer, every nerve quivering like the flying wires of his Camel.

The decoy, confident of its escort, was slowly turning towards the British lines, and this was the moment for which Biggles had been waiting, for the end of his dive would see him over his own lines — either intact or as a shattered wreck. His lips were set in a straight line under the terrific strain of the impending action as he swung inwards until the Albatroses were immediately between him and the Rumpler, and then he pointed his nose downwards. 'Come on, Batty, let's go,' he muttered huskily, and thrust the stick forward with both hands.

The top layer of Albatroses seemed to float up towards him. Five hundred feet, one hundred feet, and still they had not seen him; he could see every detail of the machines and even the faces of the pilots. He went through the middle of them like a streak of lightning — down — down — down — he knew they were hard on his heels now, but he did not look back. They would have to pull out as he went through the second layer — or risk collision. 'Come on, you swine,' he gritted through his set teeth, and went through the lower Albatroses like a thunderbolt. The Rumpler lay clear below; he could see the observer idly leaning over the side of the fuselage watching the ground. He took the machine in his sights, but held his fire, for he was still too far off for effective shooting. Down—down—down—a noise like a thousand devils shrieking in his ears, his head jammed tight against the head-rest under the frightful pressure.

At 200 feet he pressed his triggers, and his lips parted in a mirthless smile as he saw the tracers making a straight line through the centre of the Boche machine. The observer leapt round and then sank slowly on to the floor of the cockpit. The nose of the Rumpler jerked upwards, an almost certain sign that the pilot had been hit.

He held his fire until the last fraction of a second, and only when collision seemed inevitable did he pull the stick back. His under-carriage seemed to graze the centre section of the Rumpler as he came out, and he bit his lips until the blood came as he waited for the rending crash that would tell him that his wings had folded up under the pressure of that frightful zoom. Before he had reached the top of it he had thrust the stick forward again and was zig-zagging across his own lines.

For the first time since he had started the heartbursting dive he looked back. The Rumpler was nowhere in sight, but an involuntary yell broke from his lips as his eyes fell on two Albatroses, one minus its top plane, spinning wildly downwards; whether as the result of a collision or because they had cracked up in the dive, he neither knew nor cared. The five remaining Albatroses were already turning back towards their own lines, followed by a furious bombardment of archie.

Where was the Rumpler? He looked downwards. Ah! He was just in time to see it crash just behind the

British front-line trench. Tiny ant-like figures were already crawling towards it, some looking upwards, waving to him. Biggles smiled. 'Given the boys a treat, anyway,' he thought, as he pushed up his goggles and passed his hand wearily over his face. A sound like a sob was drowned in the drone of the engine. 'Well, that's that,' he said to himself, and turned his nose for home.

The following morning, as the Sergeant-Major in charge of the burying party at Lavricourt Cemetery entered the gate, his eye fell on a curious object that had been firmly planted on a new mound of earth, at the opposite end to the usual little white cross.

'What the devil's that thing, corporal?' he said, 'It wasn't there yesterday, I'll swear.'

The corporal took a few steps nearer.

'That's where they planted that R.F.C. wallah last week, Sergeant-Major,' he replied. 'Looks to me like a smashed aeroplane propeller.'

'All right, let it alone. I expect some of his pals shoved it there. For-ward—ma-arch!'

Chapter 11
The Boob

Mahoney, on his way to the sheds to take his Flight off for an early Ordinary Patrol, paused in his stride as his eye fell on Biggles leaning in an attitude of utter boredom against the door-post of the Officers' mess.

'Why so pensive, young aviator?' he smiled. 'Has Mr. Cox* grabbed your pay to square up the overdraft?' he added, as he caught sight of an open letter in the other's hand.

'Worse than that; much, much worse,' replied Biggles. 'Couldn't be worse, in fact—What do you think of this?' He held out the letter.

'I haven't time to read it, laddie. What's the trouble?'

'Oh, it's from an elderly female relative of mine. She says her son—my cousin—is in the R.F.C. on his way to France. She's pulled the wires at the Air Board for the Pool** to send him to 266, as she feels sure I can take care of him. She asks me to see that he changes his laundry regularly, doesn't drink, doesn't get mixed up with the French minxes, and a dozen other "doesn'ts." My God! it's a bit thick; what the hell does she think this is—a prep. school?'

'What's he like?'

'I don't know; it's years since I saw him; and if he's anything like the little horror he was then, God help

* Cox's were the army's official bank.
** A depot to which officers were posted until assigned to an active service squadron.

us—and him. His Christian names are Algernon Montgomery, and that's just what he looked like—a slice of warmed-up death wrapped in velvet and ribbons.'

'Sounds pretty ghastly. When's he coming?'

'To-day, apparently. His name's on the notice board. The old girl had the brass face to write to the C.O., and he's posted him to my Flight—in revenge, I expect.'

'Too bad,' replied Mahoney sympathetically. 'We'll go and get the letter done, telling her how bravely he died, and forget about it. There comes the tender now—see you later.'

Biggles, left alone, watched the tender pull up and discharge two new pilots and their kit; he had no difficulty in recognizing his new charge, who approached eagerly.

'You're Biggles—aren't you? I know you from the photo at home.'

The matured edition of the youth was even more unprepossessing than Biggles expected. His uniform was dirty, his hair long, his face, which wore a permanent expression of amused surprise, was a mass of freckles.

'My name's Captain Bigglesworth,' said the Flight-Commander coldly. 'You are posted to my Flight. Get your kit into your room, report to the Squadron office, and then come back here; I want to have a word with you.'

'Sorry, sir,' said Algernon apologetically; 'of course, I forgot.'

A few minutes later he rejoined Biggles in the mess. 'What'll you have to drink?' invited Biggles.

'Have you any ginger ale?'

'I shouldn't think so,' replied Biggles; 'we don't get

much demand for it. Have you any ginger ale, Adams?'
he asked the mess waiter—'I'll have the usual.'

'Yes, sir, I think I've got one somewhere, if I can
find it,' replied the waiter, looking at the newcomer
curiously.

'Sit down and let's talk,' said Biggles, when the
drinks had been served. 'How much flying have you
done?'

'Fourteen hours on Avros* and ten on Camels.'

'Ten hours, eh?' mused Biggles; 'ten hours. So
they're sending 'em out here with ten hours now. My
God! Now listen,' he went on, 'I want you to forget
those ten hours. This is where you'll learn to *fly*—they
can't teach you at home. If you live a week you'll begin
to know something about it. I don't want to discourage
you, but most people that come out here live on an
average twenty-four hours. If you survive a week you're
fairly safe. I can't teach you much, nobody can; you'll
find things out for yourself.

'First of all, never cross the line alone under 10,000
feet—not yet, anyway. Never go more than a couple of
miles over unless you are with a formation. Never go
down after a Hun. If you see a Hun looking like easy
meat, make for home like hell, and if that Hun fires a
Very light, kick out your foot and slam the stick over
as if somebody was already shooting at you. Act first
and think afterwards, otherwise you may not have time
to act. Never leave your formation on any account—
you'll never get back into it if you do, unless it's your
lucky day; the sky is full of Huns waiting to pile up
their scores and it's people like you that make it possible. Keep your eyes peeled and never stop looking for

* Avro 504, used extensively for training. Originally used in 1914 as a
bombing aircraft.

125

one instant. Watch the sun and never fly straight for more than two minutes at a time if you can't see what's up in the sun. Turn suddenly as if you've seen something—and you may see something. Never mind archie—it never hits anything. Watch out for balloon cables if you have to come home under 5,000. If a Hun gets on your tail, don't try to get away. Go for him. Try and bite him as if you were a mad dog; try and ram him—he'll get out of your way then. Never turn if you are meeting a Hun head-on; it isn't done. Don't shoot outside 200 feet—it's a waste of ammunition. Keep away from clouds, and, finally, keep away from balloons. It's suicide. If you want to commit suicide, do it here, because then someone else can have your bus*. If you see anything you don't understand, let it alone; never let your curiosity get the better of you. If I wave my hand above my head—make for home.** That means everybody for himself. That's all. Can you remember that?'

'I think so.'

'Right. Then let's go and have a look at the line and I'll show you the landmarks. If I shake my wings it means a Hun—I may go for it. If I do, you stay upstairs and watch me. If anything goes wrong—go straight home. When in doubt—go home, that's the motto. Got that?'

'Yes, sir.'

They took off together and circled over the aerodrome, climbing steadily for height. When his altimeter showed 6,000 feet Biggles headed for the line. It was not an

---

* Slang: aeroplane
** No aeroplanes had radio communicaton so messages between pilots were passed by hand or aeroplane movements.

ideal day for observation. Great masses of detached cumulus cloud were sailing majestically eastward and through these Biggles threaded his way, the other Camel in close attendance. Sometimes through the clouds they could see the ground, and from time to time Biggles pointed out salient landmarks—a chalk pit—stream—or wood. Gradually the recognizable features became fewer until they were lost in a scene of appalling desolation, criss-crossed with a network of fine lines scarred by pools of stagnant water.

Biggles beckoned the other Camel nearer and jabbed downwards. Explanation was unnecessary. They were looking down at no-man's-land.* Suddenly Biggles rocked his wings violently and pointed, and without further warning shot across the nose of the other Camel and dived steeply into a cloud. He pulled out underneath and looked around quickly, but of his companion there was no sign. He circled the cloud, climbing swiftly, and looking anxiously to right and left, choked back a furious curse as his eye fell on what he sought. Far away, almost out of sight in the enemy sky were five straight-winged machines; hard on their heels was a lone machine with a straight top wing and lower wings set at a dihedral angle—the Camel.

'The crazy fool,' ground out Biggles, as he set off in pursuit; but even as he watched, the six machines disappeared into a cloud and were lost to view. 'I should say that's the last anyone will see of Algernon Montgomery,' muttered Biggles philosophically, as he climbed higher, scanning the sky in the direction taken by the machines, but the clouds closed up and hid the earth from view, leaving the lone Camel the sole

* The land between the opposing armies at the front line trenches.

occupant of the sky. 'Well, I might as well go home and write that letter to his mother, as Mahoney said,' mused the pilot. 'Poor little devil! After all I told him, too. Well—!' He turned south-west and headed for home, flying by the unfailing instinct some pilots seem to possess.

Major Mullen, MacLaren and Mahoney were standing on the tarmac when he landed. 'Where's the new man, Biggles?' said Major Mullen quickly.

'He's gone,' said Biggles slowly as he took off his helmet. 'I couldn't help it, God knows. I told the young fool to stick to me like glue. We were just over the line when I spotted the shadows of five Fokkers on the clouds; I gave him the tip and went into the cloud, expecting him to follow me. When I came out he wasn't there. I went back and was just in time to see him disappearing into Hunland on the tails of the five Fokkers. I spent some time looking for him, but I couldn't find him. Could you believe that a—bah!—it's no use talking about it. I'm going for a dr—Hark!' The hum of a rotary engine rapidly approaching sent all eyes quickly upwards.

'Here he comes,' said Biggles frostily. 'Leave this to me, please, sir. I've something to say to him.'

The Camel landed and taxied in. The pilot jumped out and, with a cheerful wave of greeting, joined Biggles on the tarmac.

'I've—'

'Never mind that,' cut in Biggles curtly. 'Where the hell do you think you've been?'

'I saw the Huns—I was aching to have a crack at them—so I went after them.'

'Didn't I tell you to stay with me?'

'Yes, but—'

'Never mind "but"; you do what you're damn well told or I'll knock hell out of you. Who do you think you are—Billy Bishop or Micky Mannock*, perhaps?' sneered Biggles.

'The Huns were bolting—'

'Bolting be damned; they hadn't even seen you. If they had you wouldn't be here now. Those green and white stripes belong to von Kirtner's circus. They're killers—every one of 'em. You poor boob.'

'I got one of them.'

'*You what!*'

'I shot one down. I don't think he even saw me, though. I got all tangled up in a cloud, and when I came out and looked up his wheels were nearly on my head. I pulled my stick back and let drive right into the bottom of his cockpit. He went down. I saw the smoke against the clouds.'

Biggles subjected the speaker to a searching scrutiny. 'Where did you read that tale?' he asked slowly.

'I didn't read it, sir,' said the new pilot flushing. 'It was near a big queer-shaped wood. I think I must have been frightfully lucky.'

'Lucky!' ejaculated Biggles sarcastically. 'Lucky! Ha, ha! Lucky! You don't know how lucky you are. Now listen. If ever you leave me again I'll put you under close arrest as soon as your feet are on the ground. Whatever happens, you stick to me. I've other things to do besides write letters of condolence to your mother. All right, wash out for to-day.'

Biggles sought Major Mullen and the other Flight-

---

* Billy Bishop was a Canadian fighter pilot with 72 victories to his credit; Micky Mannock was an Irish fighter pilot with 73 victories, the highest scoring British pilot. He was killed in 1918.

Commander in the Squadron office. 'That kid got a Hun, or else he's the biggest liar on earth.'

'The liar sounds most likely to me,' observed MacLaren.

'Oh, I don't know; it has been done,' broke in Major Mullen, 'but it does seem a bit unlikely, I'll admit.'

The new pilot entered to make his report, and Biggles and MacLaren sauntered to the sheds. 'Wait a minute,' said Biggles suddenly. He swung himself into the cock-pit of the Camel which had been flown by the new pilot. 'Well, he's used his guns anyway,' he said slowly, as he climbed out again. 'I'll take him on the dawn patrol with Healy in the morning. He's not safe alone.'

Biggles, leading the two other Camels, high in the pearly morning sky, pursed his lips into a soundless whistle as his eyes fell on a charred wreck at the corner of Mossyface Wood. 'So he got him all right,' he muttered; 'the kid was right. Well I'm damned!' A group of moving specks appeared in the distance. He watched them closely for a moment, then he rocked his wings and commenced a slow turn, pointing as he did so to the enemy machines which were coming rapidly towards them. He warmed his guns, stiffened a little in his seat, and glanced to left and right to make sure that the other two Camels were in place. He saw a flash of green and white on the sides of the enemy machines as they swung round for the attack, and he unconsciously half-glanced at the new pilot. 'You'll have the dog-fight you were aching for yesterday,' was his unspoken thought. The Fokkers, six of them, were slightly above, coming straight on. Biggles lifted his nose slightly, took the leader in his sights, and waited. At 200 feet, still holding the Camel head-on to the other machines, he pressed his triggers. He saw the darting, jabbing flame of the other's guns, but did not swerve an inch. Metal spanged on metal near his face, the machine vibrated, and an unseen hand plucked at his sleeve. He clenched his teeth and held his fire. He had a swift impression of two wheels almost grazing his top plane as the first Fokker zoomed.

Out of the corner of his eye he saw Healy's tracer pouring into the Fokker at his right, and a trail of black smoke burst from the engine. Neither machine moved an inch. There was a crash which he could hear above the roar of his own engine as the Camel and the Fokker met head-on. A sheet of flame leapt upwards.

'Healy's gone—that's five to two now—not so good.' He did a lightning right-hand turn. Where was Algernon? There he was, still in position at his wing-tip. The Huns had also turned and were coming back at them. 'Bad show for a kid,' thought Biggles, and on the spur of the moment waved his left hand above his head. The pilot of the other Camel was looking at him, but made no move. 'The fool, why doesn't he go home?' Biggles muttered, as he took the nearest Fokker in his sights again and opened fire. The Hun turned and he turned behind it, and the next second all seven machines were in a complete circle. Out of the corner of his eye Biggles saw the other Camel on the opposite side of the circle on the tail of a Hun. 'Why doesn't he shoot?' Biggles cursed blindly. He pulled the stick back into his right side and shot into the circle, raking the Fokker that had opened fire on the other Camel. It zoomed suddenly, and as Biggles shot past the new pilot he waved his left arm.

He saw Algernon make a turn and dive for the line. A Fokker was on his tail instantly and Biggles raked it until it had to turn and face him. He half-rolled as a stream of lead ripped a strip of fabric from the centre section and went into a steep bank again to look at the situation.

He was alone, and there were still four Fokkers. For perhaps a minute each machine held its place in the circle, and then the Fokkers began to climb above him. Biggles knew that he was in an almost hopeless position, and he glanced around for a cloud to make a quick dash for cover, but from horizon to horizon the sky was an unbroken stretch of blue. The circle tightened as each machine strove to close it. The highest Fokker turned suddenly and dived on him, guns spitting two pencil lines of tracer. Biggles crouched a little lower in the cockpit. Two more of the Fokkers were turning on him now, and he knew that it was only a question of time before a bullet got him or his engine in a vital part.

Already the Camel was beginning to show signs of the conflict. 'God! What's that?' Biggles almost stalled as another Camel shot into the circle. It did not turn as the others, but rushed across the diameter, straight at a Fokker which jerked up in a wild zoom to avoid collision. The Camel flashed round—not in the direction of the circle, but against it, and Biggles stared open-eyed with horror as the other Fokkers shot out at a tangent to avoid disaster. 'My God! What's he doing?' he muttered, as he flung his own machine on its side to pass the other Camel. He picked out a Fokker and blazed at it. Where were the others? They seemed to be scattered all over the sky. The other Camel was circling above him. 'We'll get out of this while the going's good,' he muttered grimly, and waved his hand to the other pilot. Together they turned and dived for the line.

Biggles landed first and leant against the side of his machine to await the new pilot. For a moment he looked at him without speaking.

'Listen, laddie,' he said, when the other had joined him, 'you mustn't do that sort of thing. You'll give me the nightmare. You acted like a madman.'

'Sorry, but you told me to go for 'em like a mad dog. I thought that's what I did.'

Biggles looked at the speaker earnestly. 'Yes,' he grinned, 'that's just what you did; but why didn't you do some shooting? I never saw your tracer once.'

'I couldn't.'

'Couldn't?'

'No—my gun jammed.'

'When?'

'It jammed badly with a bulged cartridge in that first go, and I couldn't clear it.'

Biggles raised his hand to his forehead. 'Do you mean to say you came back into that hell of a dog-fight with a jammed gun?' he said slowly.

'Yes. You said stick with you.'

Biggles held out his hand. 'You'll do, kid,' he said; 'and you can call me Biggles.'

Chapter 12
The Battle of Flowers

I

The summer sun was sinking in the western sky in a blaze of crimson glory as Biggles, with his flying kit thrown carelessly over his arm, walked slowly from the sheds towards the Officers' mess. At the porch he paused in his stride to regard with wonderment the efforts of a freckled-faced youth, who, regardless of the heat, was feverishly digging up a small square patch of earth some thirty feet in front of the mess door.

'What the hell are you doing, Algy?' he called cheerfully. 'Making a private dugout for yourself?'

'No,' replied Algernon Montgomery, straightening his back with an obvious effort and wiping the perspiration off his brow with the back of his hand. 'I'm making a garden. This dust-smitten hole wants brightening up.'

'You're what?' cried Biggles incredulously.

'Making a garden, I said,' responded Algy shortly, resuming his task.

'Good God! What are you going to sow, or whatever you call it?'

'I've got some sunflowers,' replied Algy, nodding towards a newspaper package from which some wilted, sickly, green ends protruded.

'Sunflowers, eh?' said Biggles, curiously, advancing

134

towards the scene of action. 'They ought to do well. But why not plant some bananas or pineapples, or something we could eat?'

'It isn't hot enough for bananas,' said Algy, between breaths. 'They were all I could get, anyway.'

'Not hot enough?' answered Biggles. 'Holy mackerel! It feels hot enough to me to grow doughnuts.'

Algy dropped his spade and drew one of the seedlings gently from the package.

'Do you mean to tell me that you are going to stick that poor little devil in that pile of dust? I thought you said you were going to brighten things up,' said Biggles slowly.

'That'll be ten feet high presently,' said Algy confidently, scratching a hole in the earth and dropping the roots in.

'Ten feet! You mean to tell me that little squirt of a thing's got a ceiling of ten feet? Why, he's stalling already. Bah! You can't kid me. Straighten him up. You've got him a bit left wing low.'

'You push off, Biggles; I want to get these things in before dark,' cried Algy hotly. 'They've got to have some water yet.'

'They look to me as if a damn good double-Scotch would do them more good,' retorted Biggles as he turned towards the mess. 'So long, kid—see you later. You can lie up in the morning. I'll take Cowley and Tommy on the early show.'

Three hours later Biggles pushed his chair back from the card table in the anteroom. 'Well, I'm up five francs,' he announced, 'and now I'm going to roost. I'll—' A voice from the doorway interrupted him. It was Algy.

'Here, chaps,' he called excitedly, 'come and look at this—quick, before it goes.'

'He wants us to go and watch his posies sprouting in the moonlight, I expect,' grinned Biggles at Mahoney and McLaren, who were leaning back in their chairs. He turned towards the door, but as his eye fell on a window which had been flung wide open to admit as much air as possible, he stopped abruptly. 'What the hell!' he ejaculated, and sprang towards the door. The crash of falling chairs announced that the others were close behind him.

At the open doorway he stopped and looked up. A hundred feet above, a brilliant white light was sinking slowly earthwards, flooding the mess and the surrounding buildings with a dazzling radiance. A faint whistling sound, increasing in volume, became audible.

'Look out!' screamed Biggles and covering twenty yards almost in a bound dived headlong into a trench which surrounded a near-by Nissen hut. The whistle became a shrieking wail. 'Look where the hell you are coming,' yelled Biggles, as a dozen bodies thudded into the trench, one landing on the small of his back. 'Where's—' His voice was lost in a deafening detonation; a blinding sheet of flame leapt upwards.

'If they've knocked my drink over—' snarled Mahoney, struggling to get out of the trench.

'Come back, you fool,' yelled Biggles, hanging on to his foot. 'Here comes another—get down.'

Bang! Another terrific explosion shook the earth and falling debris rattled on to the tin roof beside them. The roar of an aero-engine almost on their heads, but swiftly receding, split the air.

'All right, chaps, he's gone,' said Biggles, scrambling out of the trench. 'Don't step on my cigarette case, anybody; I've dropped it somewhere. Hell's bells, he nearly caught us bending! Damn these new parachute flares, they don't give you a chance.'

'I hope he hasn't knocked our wine store sideways, like somebody did to 55 the other day,' grumbled Mahoney. 'Hullo! the searchlights have got him. Just look at that stinking archie; I wouldn't be in that kite for something.'

All eyes were turned upwards to where a black-crossed machine was twisting and turning in the beams of three searchlights which had fastened upon it. The air around was torn with darting, crimson jets of flame.

'He'll get away; they always do,' said MacLaren with deep disgust, making his way towards the mess.

'Well, I hope he does; he deserves to. I'd hate his job,' observed Biggles philosophically.

'Where's Algy?'

'I expect the kid's gone to see if his plantation's all right,' replied Mahoney. 'Well, good-night, chaps—good-night, Biggles.'

'Cheerio, laddie.'

Ten minutes later there was a knock on Biggles' door, and in reply to his invitation a wild-eyed, freckled-faced youth thrust his head inside. He seemed to be labouring under some great emotion.

'What—what was that?' he gasped.

Biggles grinned. 'Hanoverana—didn't you see it in the beam?' he replied. 'There's no harm done.'

'Where did that dirty dog come from, do you think?' choked Algy.

'Aerodrome 29, I expect, they are the only Hanovers near here. Must have crossed the line at twenty thousand and glided down with his engine off,' replied Biggles.

'Where's Aerodrome 29?'

'On, go to the map-room and find out; it's time you knew. There are some photos there, too. Push off, I'm tired and I'm on the early show.'

Algy stood for a moment breathing heavily, staring at his Flight-Commander, and then abruptly slammed the door.

II

Biggles scarcely seemed to have closed his eyes when he was awakened by the ear-splitting roar of an engine. It was still dark. He grabbed his luminous watch and looked at the time—it was 3.30. 'What the devil—' he croaked, springing out of bed. He reached the window just as the dim silhouette of a Camel passed overhead. He flung on a dressing-gown and raced along the sun-baked path to the sheds. 'Who's that just gone off?' he called to a tousled-headed ack-emma who was still staring upwards with a vacant grin on his face.

'Alger—sorry, sir—Mr—'

'Never mind,' snapped Biggles, overlooking the breach of respect, 'I know. Where's he gone—did he say?'

'No, sir, but I saw him marking up his map. He took eight Cooper bombs.'

'What did he mark on his map?' snapped Biggles.

'Aerodrome 29, sir.'

Biggles swung on his heel and tore back towards the huts. He shook and pummelled the life into Cowley and Thomas. 'Come on,' he said tersely, 'jump to it. Algy's gone off his rocker—he's shooting up 29 alone. Let's get away.'

Sidcots were hastily donned over pyjamas, and

within five minutes three machines were in the air heading for the line. The sun was creeping up over the horizon when Biggles, at 5,000 feet, waved to the other two pilots and leaning over the side of his cockpit, pointed downwards. Far below, a tiny moving speck was circling and banking over a line of hangars. A cloud of white smoke arose into the air. Tiny ant-like figures were running to and fro.

'The fool, the crazy lunatic,' gasped Biggles, as he pushed the stick forward and went roaring down with the others behind him. At 500 feet a row of holes appeared like magic in his wing and he sideslipped violently. He levelled out and poured a stream of tracer at a group of figures clustered around a machine-gun. A green machine was taking off cross-wind; he swung down behind it and raked it with a stream of lead. The gunner in the rear seat dropped limply and the machine crashed into the trees at the far end of the aerodrome. The air was full of the rattle of guns and an ominous flack! flack! flack! behind warned him that it was time to be leaving.

He looked around for Algy, and, spotting him still circling, zoomed across his nose, frantically waving his arm above his head. 'If he doesn't come now he can stay and get what he deserves,' muttered Biggles, as he shot over the edge of the aerodrome. He looked behind. To his relief three Camels were on his tail, so, climbing swiftly for height, he headed back towards the lines.

'I'll see him back home and then go straight on with the morning show,' he mused a few minutes later as they raced across the lines in a flurry of archie. He landed and leaned against the side of the Camel while he waited for the others to come in. Another Camel

139

touched its wheels gently on the aerodrome and finished its run not twenty yards away. Algy sprang out of the cockpit and ran towards him. 'I got it—I got it!' he shouted exultantly as he ran.

'Who do you think you are?' snapped Biggles, 'Archimedes?'

'I got four hits out of eight,' cried Algy joyously.

'You got nothing—I had a good look. You didn't touch a single hangar,' growled Biggles.

'Hangar—hangar—' replied Algy stupidly, 'who's talking about hangars?'

'I am, what else do you suppose?'

'Hangars be damned!' cried Algy, 'I mean their geraniums!'

'Germaniums—germaniums—my God, am I going crazy—what are you talking about—germaniums?'

'Raniums—raniums—N—N—! Good Lord! Did you never hear of geraniums? They had a bed full of geraniums and calceolarias.'

'Calcium—calcium—' Biggles took a quick step backwards and whipped out his Very pistol. 'Here, stand back you or I'll shoot. You're daft.'

'Daft be damned! I mean flowers—I've scattered their blinking geraniums all over the aerodrome.'

Biggles stared at him for a moment, his jaw sagging foolishly. 'Do you mean to tell me you've been to that hell-hole, and dragged me there to bomb a ruddy flowerbed?'

'Yes, and I've made a salad of their lettuce patch,' added Algy triumphantly.

'But why? What have the lettuces done to you?'

'Done to me? Haven't you seen what that damn swine did to my sunflowers last night?'

140

Biggles swung round on his heel as enlightenment burst upon him. At the spot where Algy's flower-bed had been yawned a deep round hole.

Chapter 13
The Bomber

Biggles, cruising along the line on a dawn patrol, pressed on the rudder-bar with his left foot as his ever-searching eyes fell on a line of white archie bursts to the south-east, far over the British lines. The colour of the bursts told him at once that the shells were being fired by British guns, for German anti-aircraft gunfire was usually black. It could only mean that one or more enemy machines were in the vicinity, an event sufficiently unusual to intrigue him immensely. 'I must look into this,' was his unspoken thought as he headed his Camel along a course which would intercept the target of the rapidly-lengthening line of archie bursts.

A small, black speck, well in front of the foremost bursts, soon became visible and his curiosity increased, for the machine was of a type unknown to him. As he drew nearer a puzzled frown lined his forehead.

'I don't believe it; it can't be true,' he murmured at last, when only a few hundred yards separated him from his objective. The anti-aircraft fire ceased when the gunners observed his presence, and Biggles closed rapidly with the other machine, which with sublime indifference continued on its way without paying the slightest attention to him. Large Maltese crosses on the tail and fuselage left no doubt as to its nationality.*

It was the largest aeroplane Biggles had ever seen.

* Some German aeroplanes in the First World War were painted with the Maltese Cross (see front cover of *Biggles of the Fighter Squadron*).

He noted two engines, one on each side of the fuselage, and raked his memory for some rumour or gossip by which he could identify it. 'It isn't a Gotha*,' he mused; 'damned if I know what it is; but I'll bet she carries a tidy load of eggs.' Almost unconsciously he had been edging nearer to the nose of the big machine as he inspected it, but a sudden burst of fire from the gunner in the nacelle**, and an ominous flack! flack flack! behind warned him that the crew were on the alert and well prepared to receive him. He made a lightning right-hand turn, and as he flashed back past the bomber a murderously accurate burst of fire from the rear gunner startled him still further. 'Hell's bells!' swore Biggles, 'this is a bit hot.'

The big machine had not moved an inch from its course, and to be thus treated with contempt annoyed him intensely. They were rapidly approaching the lines and if he was to prevent the return of the bomber to its aerodrome, something would have to be done quickly.

Biggles swept to the rear of the machine, swearing again as the Camel bumped violently in the slipstream of the two engines. 'All right, let's see how you like this one,' he snapped angrily, and put his nose down in a steep dive. He was following the usual practice of attacking a two-seater, judging his speed and distance to bring him up under the elevators of the enemy machine, out of the field of fire of both gunners.

The attack was perfectly timed and the Camel soared up like a bird immediately under the big fuselage. Biggles glanced through the sights and took the bomber

* German twin-engined biplane with a crew of three, which carried 14 bombs weighing a maximum total of 1100 lbs.
** The crew section placed on or between the wings.

at where he judged the pilot's seat to be, withholding his fire until the Camel was almost at stalling point in order to make certain of his aim. What happened next occurred with startling rapidity. The muzzles of a pair of twin Parabellum guns slid out of a trap door in the floor of the bomber and the next instant a double stream of lead was shooting the Camel to pieces about him. Flack! flack! Whang! whang! sang the bullets as they bored through fabric and metal. Biggles, shaken as never before in all his flying experience, kicked out his left foot spasmodically and flung the stick over and back into his stomach. The Camel whirled over and fell into a dive; the 150 h.p. Bentley Rotary coughed once—twice—and then cut out altogether. The propeller stopped dead and the thoroughly alarmed pilot started to glide earthwards with the rapidly-diminishing hum of the bomber's engines in his ears.

Biggles pushed up his goggles and looked downwards, and then up at the fast disappearing Boche machine.

'Phew! My God' he muttered soberly, 'that'll stop me laughing in church in the future. What a hell-trap. Who would have guessed it? Well, we live and learn,' he concluded bitterly, and turned his attention to the inevitable forced landing. He anticipated no difficulty, for he had ample height from which to choose a landing ground. 'Thank goodness I'm over my own side of the line,' he mused philosophically, as he slowly lost height.

He could not get to his own aerodrome, at Maranique, but 287 Squadron might just be reached, and although he did not look forward with any degree of pleasure to the inevitable jibes of the S.E.5 pilots, it was better than risking damaging the machine in an open field.

He made a good landing in the middle of the aerodrome and sat up on the 'hump' of the Camel to await the arrival of the mechanics to tow the machine to the tarmac, where a group of cheering pilots awaited him.

'Get stung, Biggles?' yelled Wilkinson, the good-natured Flight Commander.

'I got stung all right,' acknowledged Biggles ruefully. 'That kite's got more stings than a hornet's nest. What the hell is it, anyway?'

'That's our pet Friedrichshafen.* Come and have a drink while we ring up your old man and tell him you're O.K., and I'll tell you about it,' said Wilks, linking his arm through that of the Camel pilot's.

'Have you had a go at it?' inquired Biggles.

'Me? We've all had a go at it. It comes over just before dawn nearly every day, lays its eggs, and beetles home about this time.'

'And do you mean to say that you can't stop it?' exclaimed Biggles incredulously.

Wilkinson shrugged his shoulders. 'You didn't do a hell of a lot yourself, did you. The only thing that did any stopping was your cowling by the look of it. It's as full of holes as a colander. It'd be easier to sink a battleship than that flying arsenal. There isn't a blind spot anywhere that we've discovered; the usual weak spots aren't weak any longer. They just plaster you whichever way you come—oh!—I know. Twin mobile guns'll beat fixed guns any day. I'm not aching to commit suicide, so I let it alone, and that's a fact. There was a rumour that Wing had offered three pips to anybody who got it. Lacie of 281 had a go, and went down in flames. Crickson of 383 had a stab at it in one

---

* Twin-engined biplane bomber with a crew of three. It could carry a bomb-load of 3000 lbs.

of the new Dolphins*, and it took a week to dig him out of the ground. Most people keep their distance now and watch archie do its daily dozen, but *they* couldn't hit a damn Zeppelin at fifty yards. Guns** reckons that the Friedrichshafen costs our people who are paying for the War, five thousand pounds a day for archie ammunition, and I reckon he isn't far out.'

'I see,' said Biggles thoughtfully. 'Well, I'll be getting back if you can find me transport. I'll come back for the Camel later on. Cheerio, Wilks.'

'Cheerio, Biggles. Keep away from that Hun till the first of the month. I'll send you a wreath, but I'm broke till then.'

'Yes? Well, don't chuck your money away on losers. What you'll need is a pair of spectacles next time I meet that Hun.'

After seeing the damaged Camel brought home, and the ignition lead which had caused the engine failure repaired, Biggles spent the evening with a lead pencil and some paper, making drawings of the big bomber as he remembered it. He marked the three guns and drew lines and circles to represent the field of fire covered by each. He quickly discovered that what Wilkinson had told him concerning the guns covering all angles of approach was correct, and ordinary attack was almost useless, and certainly very dangerous.

The old weakness in the defence of all big machines, which was underneath the fuselage, did not exist. The only possible spot which could be regarded as 'blind'

* British Sopwith Dolphin—biplane fighter armed with two machine guns, in service 1917. Not as popular as the Camel— it was only used by 4 RAF squadrons.
** Guns was the usual squadron nickname for the gunnery officer.

was immediately under the nacelle, and even so he would be exposed to the fire of at least one of the gunners while he was manoeuvring into that position. He considered the possibility of dropping bombs, but discarded it as impraticable. If he dropped the bombs over his own side of the line and missed, the people down below would have something to say about it, and it was hardly likely that he would be allowed to go about it unmolested over the German side.

No! The only chance was the spot under the nacelle and then to use a Lewis gun which fired upwards through his centre section. He did not usually carry this weapon, as he infinitely preferred head-on tactics with his double Vickers guns; not entirely satisfied with the result of his calculations, he gave instructions for the Lewis gun to be fitted, told his batman* to call him an hour before dawn, and went to bed.

It was still dark when, with his flying coat and boots over his pyjamas, he climbed into the cockpit of his Camel the following morning. He felt desperately tired and disinterested in the project, and half regretted his decision to pursue it, but once in the air he felt better.

It was a glorious morning. A few late stars still lingered in the sky; to the east the first gleam of dawn was lightening the horizon. He pointed his nose and cruised steadily in the direction of his encounter of the preceding day, climbing steadily and inhaling the fresh morning air. As he climbed, the rim of the sun, still invisible to those below, crept up over the skyline and bathed the Camel in an orange glow. Around and below him the earth was a vast basin of indigo and deep purple shadows, stretching, it seemed, to eternity.

*An attendant serving an officer. A position discontinued in today's RAF.

He appeared to hang over the centre of it, an infinitesimal speck in a strange world in which no other living creature moved. The sense of utter loneliness and desolation, well known to pilots, oppressed him, and he was glad when six D.H.9's, that had crept up unseen from the void beneath, gleamed suddenly near him like jewels on velvet as the rays of the sun flashed on their varnished wings. He flew closer to them and waved to the observers, leaning idly over their Scarff rings.* The Nines held on their way and were soon lost in the mysterious distance. Biggles idly wondered how many of them would come back. The dome above him had turned pale green, and then turquoise, not slowly, but quickly, as if hidden lights had been switched on by the master of a stage performance.

'And this is war!' mused the pilot. 'God! it's hard to believe—but unless I'm mistaken here it comes,' he added, as his eye caught a cluster of tiny sparks in the far distance at about his own height. 'Good morning, Archibald, you dirty dog,' he muttered, as he eyed the approaching flashes at the head of which he could now discern the silhouette of the big bomber. He swiftly closed the distance between them, warming his guns as he went, and the answering stream of tracer from the forward guns of the bomber brought a faint smile to his lips. There was no chance of approaching unobserved and he had not attempted it. He circled slowly 500 feet above the big machine and looked down; the gunner in the rear cockpit gave him a mock salute, and he waved back.

He wasted no further time on pleasantries, but dived steeply, still well outside effective range. Down and

*The gun mounting which completely encircled the gunner's cockpit. Around this ring the gun could slide to point in any direction.

148

down he went until he was well below the bomber and then slowly pulled the stick back; the bomber seemed to be dropping out of the sky on to him. He was coming up under the nacelle and his eyes were glued to the trap door through which he could see the crouching gunner. A spurt of flame leapt outwards towards him and the ominous tell-tale flack! flack! flack! behind and on each side told that the gunner was making good shooting. A moment later he was flying on even keel not more than twenty feet below the nacelle and in the same direction as the other machine.

Something seemed to drop off the bomber and whizz past him; he looked upwards with a start in time to see another bomb swing off the bomb-rack and hurtle past dangerously near. He looked along the line of racks, but could see no more bombs, which relieved him greatly, for he had entirely overlooked the fact that the bomber might not have laid all its eggs. He could see the face of the forward gunner peering over the side, looking at him, and a quick glance astern revealed spasmodic bursts of tracer passing harmlessly under the tail of the Camel. Satisfied that the gunner could not reach him, he took the joystick between his knees and seized his top gun, left hand grasping the spade-grip and right forefinger curled around the trigger. Rat-tat—he cursed luridly as he struggled to clear the jammed gun. Why did guns always jam at the crucial moment?

The bomber was turning now and he had to grab the stick with one hand to keep his place. He stood up in the cockpit and hammered at the ammunition drum with his fist. He tried the trigger, found the gun was working and, dropping back into his seat, just had time to push the stick forward as the bomber came down

149

on him as its pilot tried to tear his wing off with its undercarriage. He sideslipped in a wild attempt to keep in position, but his windscreen flew to pieces as a stream of tracer from the rear gun caught him. He dived frantically away, kicking alternate feet as he went to spoil the gunner's aim.

Safely out of range he pushed up his goggles and wiped his forehead. 'Damn this for a game,' he moaned, 'but for that jam I'd have had him then.' He glanced down and was horrified to see that they were already over the enemy lines. He tested his top gun to make sure that it was working and then savagely repeated his manoeuvre to come up underneath the bomber. He held his breath as he ran the gauntlet of the gunners again, and then at point-blank range he dropped the stick, seized the gun and pressed the trigger.

There was no mistake this time. He held the burst until the Camel began to fall away from under him and then he dropped back into his seat grabbing wildly at the stick as the machine went into a spin, bracing himself with all his strength against the sides of the cockpit to prevent himself being thrown out.

'My God! That's all I want of that,' he muttered, as he got the machine under control and looked around for the bomber.

It was steering an erratic course for the ground, obviously in difficulties. He dived after it and noticed that the rear gunner's cockpit was empty. 'I've hit the pilot and the observer is trying to get the machine down,' he decided instantly, and a closer view confirmed his suspicions, for he could see the observer holding the joystick over the shoulder of the limp figure of the pilot.

'I hope he manages it,' thought Biggles anxiously,

and held his hand up to show that they had nothing more to fear from him, afterwards circling round to watch the landing. It was a creditable effort; the big machine flattened out, but failed to clear a line of trees; Biggles almost fancied he could hear the crash as it settled down in a pile of torn fabric and splintered wood.

'I'll have to go and tell Wilks about this,' said the elated pilot to himself, as he steered a course for the S.E.5 aerodrome; 'he'll be tickled to death!'

Chapter 14
On Leave

Captain Bigglesworth glanced up carelessly at the notice-board in passing; a name caught his eye and he took a step nearer. The name was his own:

Captain J. C. Bigglesworth. Posted to 69 F.T.S.*
Narborough. W./48 P./1321.

he read. For a full minute he looked at the notice uncomprehendingly, and as its full significance dawned upon him, swore savagely and hurried to the Squadron office.

'Yes, Biggles,' said Major Mullen glancing up from his desk, 'do you want to see me?'

'I see I'm posted to Home Establishment,' replied Biggles. 'May I ask why?'

The C.O. laid down his pen, crossed the room and laid a fatherly hand on the Flight-Commander's shoulder. 'I'm sorry, Biggles,' he said simply, 'but I've got to send you home. Now listen to me. I've been out here longer than you have. I know every move in the game; that's why I'm commanding 266. I know when a man's cracking up; I saw you start weeks ago; when Batson went West you were at breaking point. Now, remember I'm telling you this for your own good—not to hurt your feelings. I think too much of you for that.

---

* Flying Training School, based in the UK.

If I thought less of you, why, I'd leave you here to go on piling up the score in the Squadron "game book." If you did stay here, you'd be a sot in a month. Already you're drinking more than you used to; that's the beginning of the end. You'll be caught napping; you'll stall taking-off, or you'll hit a tree coming in. Cleverer pilots than you have gone out that way. You can't help it and you can't stop it. No one can stand the pace for ever. This game makes an old man of a young one without him knowing it. That's the truth, Biggles. You've got to have a rest. If you don't rest now you'll never be able to rest again. You are more use to us alive than dead; put it that way if you like. That's why I put your posting through.'

'But can't I have a rest without being posted?' said Biggles bitterly.

'No, I have asked you to take some leave. The M.O. has asked you, and I've heard Mac and Mahoney telling you to—they've both been on leave and it's done them a power of good.'

'All right, sir. I'll go on leave if you'll cancel the posting. It would kill me to hang about an F.T.S.'

'Very well. Fill in your application. Ten days with effect from to-morrow. I'll send it to Wing by hand right away. You stay on the strength of 266.'

'I've only one other thing to ask, sir. May I fly home?'

'There you go, you see. You can't leave it alone. Well, you might get a lift with a ferry pilot from Bourget. How's that?'

'Not for me,' said Biggles firmly. 'I'm not trusting my life to any ferry pilot. I'll fly myself in a Camel.'

'How am I going to account for the Camel if you break it up?'

'Break it! I don't break machines up.'

'You might.'

'Well, send one back for reconditioning. I'll take it.'

'All right,' said the C.O. after a brief pause. 'It's against regulations and you know it. Don't come back here without that Camel, that's all.'

'Very good, sir.'

Biggles saluted briskly and departed.

Major Mullen turned to 'Wat' Tyler, the Recording Officer, who had been a witness of the scene, and deliberately winked. 'You were right, Tyler,' he smiled. 'That posting worked the trick; that was the only way we would have got him to take some leave.'

Early the following morning Biggles, in his best uniform, took off and steered a course for Marquise, where he proposed to refuel before crossing the Channel. He eyed the enemy sky longingly, but true to his word to the C.O., held firmly to his way. The trip proved uneventful, and midday found him lunching in the officers' mess at Lympne. He reported to the officer commanding the station, presented his movement order, saw his machine safely in a hangar, and went on to London by train.

Arriving home, he discovered the house closed; he telephoned a friend of the family, only to find out that his father and brother, his only living relations, were in the Army and 'somewhere in France.' 'Well, that's that,' said Biggles as he hung up the receiver. 'I might have known they would be.'

For a week he hung about town, thoroughly bored, doing little except drift between his hotel, the Long Bar at the Trocadero, the American Bar at the Alhambra, or anywhere he thought he might strike somebody he knew, home on leave from the Front. The weather was cold and wet and he looked forward joyfully to his return to the Squadron. And then, walking down Shaftesbury Avenue, he met Dick Harboard, his father's greatest friend and business associate. Over a drink Biggles briefly explained his position, bitterly lamenting the time he was wasting when he might be doing something useful in France. 'I'm sick of loafing about here,' he concluded. 'London is getting me down fast. I hate the sight of the place, but there's nowhere else to go.'

'Why not come down to my place for the rest of your time. I've a shooting party down for the week-end. Mixed crowd, of course— some funny people have got the money these days, but it can't be helped. What about it?'

'Where is your place?'

'Felgate, in Kent—near Folkestone.'

'Folkestone is near Lympne, isn't it?'

'Next door to it. Why?'

'Oh, I just wondered,' said Biggles vaguely. He did not think it worth while explaining that he had a machine at Lympne and had visions of putting in a few hours' flying-time if the weather improved.

'Good enough,' said Harboard as they parted. 'I shall expect you to-night in time for dinner.'

'I'll be along,' agreed Biggles. 'I'll come down in mufti* I think, and forget the war for a bit. Cheerio— see you later.'

Biggles, clad in grey flannels and a sweater, deep in a Sabatini novel from his host's library, paused to pull

* Out of uniform.

his chair a little nearer to the hall fire. It was bitterly cold for the time of the year; lowering skies and a drizzle of rain had put all ideas of flying out of his head, and he settled down for a comfortable spell of reading.

He frowned as the door opened to admit a party of men and girls whose heavy boots and macintoshes proclaimed them to be a shooting party, bound for the fields. At their head was Frazer, a big, florid, middle-aged man to whom Biggles had taken an instant dislike when they had been introduced the previous evening. Biggles did not like the easy air of familiarity with which he had addressed him. His loud overbearing manner, particularly when there were women present, irritated his frayed nerves. He had noticed on arrival that none of the party were in uniform, and he wondered vaguely why a man of such obviously splendid physique as Frazer was not in the Army; to save any possible embarrassment he had asked to be introduced as Mr Bigglesworth. He was not left long in wonder, for Frazer, tapping his chest ruefully with his forefinger, complained at frequent intervals of the weak heart that kept him at home and thus prevented him from showing in actual practice how the War could be ended forthwith.

The fact that he was obviously making a lot of money out of the War did nothing to lessen Biggles' irritation, and these were the reasons why he had decided to remain in the hall with a book rather than have to suffer the fellow's society with the shooting party.

'Well, well,' observed Frazer in affected surprise with his eyes on the slippers on Biggles's feet. 'Not coming out with the guns?'

'No, thanks,' replied Biggles civilly.

156

'Huh! I should have thought a bit of exercise would have done you good; a shot or two at the birds will get your eye in for when you join the Army.' The sneer behind the words was unmistakable.

'It's too confoundedly cold, and I hate getting my feet wet,' said Biggles quietly, keeping his temper with an effort.

'I can't understand you young fellows,' went on Frazer, when the snigger that had followed Biggles' words had subsided. 'Anyway, I should have thought there were plenty of things you could do with a War on besides rotting over a fire.'

Again the inference was obvious, and Biggles choked back a hot retort. 'Bah! Why argue,' was his unspoken thought. The man was in his element, holding the floor; well, let him. He eyed Frazer coldly, without answering, and it may have been something in his eye that caused Frazer to shift uneasily and turn to the outside door.

'Well, let's get along, folks,' he said loudly. 'Somebody has got to keep the home fires burning, I suppose,' was his parting shot as the door closed behind them.

Biggles, left alone, smiled to himself for a moment, and then settled down to his book. The telephone in the next room shrilled noisily—again, and yet again, and Biggles breathed a prayer of thankfulness when he heard Lea, the butler, answer it. He was half-way through the first chapter of his book when the 'phone again jarred his nerves with its insistent jangle. He laid down his book with a weary sigh. 'My God! I can't stand this infernal racket,' he muttered, and looked up to see Lea standing white-faced in the doorway.

'What's the matter, Lea?' he asked irritably, 'is the house on fire or something?'

'No, sir; but Mr. Harboard is out. He is the Chief Constable you know, and they say that two German seaplanes are bombing Ramsgate.'

'What!' Biggles leapt up as if he had been stung by a hornet. 'Say that again.'

'Two German seaplanes—'

Biggles made a flying leap to the window and cast a critical eye at the sky. The rain had stopped and small patches of blue showed through the scudding clouds.

'Quick!' he snapped, every nerve tingling with excitement, 'get the car round.'

The butler, shaken from his normal sedate bearing by the brisk command, departed almost at a run.

'Get me to Lympne as quickly as you can; put your foot down and keep it down,' he told the chauffeur a few minutes later, as, with flying coat, cap and goggles over his arm, he jumped into the big saloon car.

For fifteen minutes Biggles fretted and fumed with impatience as the car tore through the narrow Kentish lanes. 'Go on,' he shouted, when they arrived at the aerodrome, 'straight up to the hanger.'

The guard at the gate challenged him, but Biggles yelled him aside with a swift invective.

'Get that Camel out of No. 3 shed,' he snapped at a group of idling mechanics. 'Number 9471—jump to it!' and then he burst into the C.O.'s office.

'Captain Bigglesworth, 266 Squadron, on leave from overseas, sir. You remember I reported last week?'

'Oh, yes, I remember,' said the C.O. 'What's the hurry?'

'Two Huns are bombing Ramsgate—I'm going for them. I've got ammunition—I had two belts put in in case I ran into anything coming over.'

'But—'

Biggles was already on his way; he took a flying leap into the cockpit.

'Switches off, petrol on,' sang out the ack-emma.

'Petrol on,' echoed Biggles.

'Contact!'

'Contact!'

The Bentley started with a roar and sent a cloud of smoke whirling aft in the slipstream. He adjusted his goggles, waved the chocks away, and a few minutes later was in the air heading N.N.E. with the coastline cutting across the leading edge of his starboard wing. He had no maps, but he estimated the distance to Ramsgate to be about fifteen to twenty miles, not more; with the wind under his tail he should be there in less than ten minutes. Deal was on his starboard quarter now, and Sandwich loomed ahead; in the distance he could see the sweep in the coast where the North Foreland jutted out.

He had been flying low in order to watch the landmarks, but now he pulled the joystick back and climbed through a convenient hole in the clouds. Above, the cloud-tops were bathed in brilliant sunshine, and still climbing, he looked eagerly ahead for the enemy machines. The only machine he could see was an old F.E. circling aimlessly some distance inland, so he pointed his nose north-west and headed out to sea in an endeavour to cut the raiders off should they have started on the homeward journey.

For a quarter of an hour he flew thus, peering ahead and around him for the hostile machines. Doubts began to assail him. Suppose the whole thing was a wild rumour? What a fool he had been not to get some reliable information before he started. His altimeter was registering 10,000 feet, the clouds, through which he could occasionally see patches of grey sea, were far below.

He commenced a wide circle back towards land, noting that he had already ventured much too far away to be safe should his engine give trouble. He throttled back to three-quarter and for a few minutes cruised quietly in a due easterly direction, touching his rudder-bar from time to time to permit a clear view ahead.

A movement—or was it instinct—made him glance to the north. Far away, flying close together were two machines—seaplanes. He was round in an instant heading north-west to cut them off. Five minutes later he could see that he would catch them, for they were appreciably nearer. He could tell the moment they saw him, for they turned in a more northerly direction away from him and put their noses down for more speed. A few minutes later he could see the black crosses and the gunners standing up waiting to receive him. 'Well, mused Biggles, 'this is no place to mess about in a Camel. If I run out of fuel, or if they get a shot in my tank, I'm sunk. I must have been crazy to come right out here. It's neck or nothing if I'm going to do anything. Here goes.'

He pushed his nose down for speed and then pulled up in a steep zoom under the elevators of the nearest machine; but the pilot had seen his move and swung broadside on and exposed him to the full view of his gunner who at once opened fire; but his shooting was wild, and Biggles could see his tracer passing harmlessly some distance away. The Camel pilot deliberately hung back until the other had emptied his drum of ammunition and started to replace it with a new one; then he zoomed in to point-blank range, and, knowing that he might not get such another opening, held his fire until his sights were aligned on the forward cockpit, and then pressed his triggers.

The nose of the Brandenburg* seaplane tilted sharply upwards, and then dropped; the machine made an aimless half-turn that quickly became a spin as the nose dropped, and then whirled downwards with the engine still at full throttle.

Biggles fell off on to his wing and peered through his centre section for the second seaplane. For a moment he could not see it and when he did spot it, it was going down in a steep dive towards the clouds. 'Looks as if he's lost his nerve,' muttered the Camel pilot as he pushed his stick forward and went down like a thunderbolt in the wake of the diving German.

He opened fire some distance away at a range which he knew quite well could not be effective unless a lucky shot found its mark, but he did it with the deliberate intention of rattling an obviously nervous foe.

The Brandenburg dropped tail-up into the cloud-bank and Biggles carefully followed it; he found it again just below the clouds and resumed the chase. Just ahead, a wide patch of blue sky showed through a gap in the cloud and Biggles closed in quickly, but the German swung round in obvious indecision. 'The fool can't be thinking of trying to land,' thought Biggles in astonishment, and fired a series of short bursts to confuse his opponent still more. But the German had had enough, and apparently having no wish to share the fate of his companion, cut off his engine and commenced to glide down towards the water. A new possibility occurred to Biggles. 'If he gets that kite down on the water safely the gunner might be able to hold me

* German two-seater seaplane used for reconnaissance and light bombing.

off until my petrol ran out,' he thought. He also knew that a floating target was more difficult to hit than one in the air, for he dare not risk overshooting his mark. 'Well, I've got to cramp his style,' thought Biggles, and he dived recklessly at the seaplane, guns streaming tracer, to which, to his surprise, the enemy gunner made no reply.

'What a gutless hound,' he thought. 'Hullo—there he goes!'

The Brandenburg pilot, in his haste to get out of that withering blast of lead, had tried to land too fast; the floats struck the surface of the sea with a terrific splash, the nose buried itself under the water and the tail cocked high into the air. Biggles watched both occupants climb along to the elevators, and, circling low, pointed in the direction of the shore, in the hope that they would realize that he had gone for help.

'You are wanted on the 'phone, sir,' said Lea, the butler, apologetically.

It was late in the afternoon. Biggles put down his book and hurried to the instrument, for he was expecting the call, and anxious to hear the fate of the two German airmen. He picked up the receiver.

'Major Sidgrove speaking, from Lympne,' said a voice.

'Captain Bigglesworth here, sir,' replied Biggles.

'Good show, Bigglesworth; we found both machines in the sea. The crew of the first were both dead— gunshot wounds, but the others were all right except for shock and exposure. Rather funny; the pilot had a brace of beautiful black eyes that the observer had given him. The pilot was an N.C.O. under the command of an officer in the rear seat; the Germans fly like that, you know.'

Biggles knew well enough, but he made no comment.

'Apparently it was the pilot's first show,' went on the Major, 'and when you started shooting he went to bits. He made for the water with the officer beating hell out of him and yelling for him to get into the clouds. He was swiping him over the nut instead of shooting at you. I've never seen a man so peeved in my life. Well, that's all. I thought you'd like to know. I've forwarded your report to the Ministry. They've been on the phone wanting to know what the dickens you were doing at Lympne, where you got the Camel, who gave you instructions, and God knows what else! They seem more concerned about that than about the two Huns—they would be! I expect they'll send for you during the next day or two; where can I get hold of you if they do?'

'Maranique,' replied Biggles shortly. 'I'm going back to-morrow. Many thanks, Major; good-bye.'

Biggles hung up the receiver and returned to the hall. The door opened and the shooting party, covered with mud, entered. Frazer looked at Biggles in undisguised disgust.

'Still keeping the fire warm,' he sneered. 'You should have been with us, we've had great sport.'

'So have I,' said Biggles softly.

'I got in some pretty shooting,' continued Frazer.

'Funny, so did I,' said Biggles smiling faintly.

'You! Why you haven't been out. I can't understand why some people are so careful about their skins.'

One of the girls came forward.

'There,' she said, 'I've brought you a little souvenir.' She laid a small white feather* on the table.

* A symbol of cowardice.

'Thanks,' said Biggles evenly, 'I've always wanted a feather in my cap. I've got one to-day.'

Mr. Harcourt bustled into the room.

'What's that—what's that—feather in your cap? I should say it will be. I shouldn't be surprised if you got the D.S.O.* Well done, my boy, you deserve it.'

'D.S.O.—D.S.O.—' echoed Frazer stupidly, 'What the devil for?'

'Haven't you heard?'

'Oh, cut it out, sir,' protested Biggles.

'Cut it out, be damned. I'm proud to have you under my roof and I want everybody to know it.' He turned to the others. 'He's just shot down a couple of Hun bombers in the sea, after they had bombed Ramsgate.'

A silence fell that could almost be felt.

'Who—who is he?' blurted out Frazer, at last, nodding towards Biggles, who was lighting a cigarette. 'He's not *the* Bigglesworth—the fellow we read about in the papers—the flyer—is he?'

'Of course he is; who else did you think he was?' cried Harcourt in astonishment.

'Well,' said Frazer quietly, 'I'll be getting along. I've just had a phone call calling me up to Newcastle in the morning. I'll have to start to-night to catch my train.'

'That's all right,' said Biggles cheerfully. 'Stay the night and I'll fly you up in the morning. I can get a Bristol from Lympne.'

'No, thanks,' replied Frazer firmly.

'I can't understand some people,' said Biggles softly, as he turned towards the library, 'being so careful about their skins.'

---

* Distinguished Service Order, a medal.

Chapter 15
Fog!

Fog, mist, and still more mist. Biggles crouched lower in his cockpit as the white vapour swirled aft, and wished he had taken Major Sidgrove's advice and waited at Lympne until it had lifted.

'It will clear as the sun comes up,' he had told the Major, optimistically, as he took off. He was anxious to get back to the Squadron, and although visibility on the ground had not been good, he did not think it was so bad as it proved to be in the air. At 500 feet the ground was completely hidden from view, but a glance at the compass told him that he was heading towards the French coast. 'What a hell of a day!' he muttered, and climbed steadily to get above the opaque curtain. At 5,000 feet the mist began to thin and the sun showed wanly as a pale white orb; when his altimeter told him that he was 6,000 feet above the earth, he emerged into clear sunshine with a suddenness that was startling.

'I've a damn poor chance of finding the aerodrome if this stuff doesn't lift,' he told himself as he skimmed along just above the pea-soup vapour. For an hour he followed his course, peering below anxiously for a break in the mist to show him his whereabouts, but in vain. 'Well, I'd better go down and see where I am,' he muttered; he throttled back and slid once more into the bank of clammy moisture. He was flying blind now, hoping against hope that the mist would thin out before he reached the ground; if it didn't, well, he would probably crash, that's all there was to it; but sooner or later he would have to come down, and he preferred to do it now rather than when he was getting short of fuel.

He kept a watchful eye on the altimeter; 2,000—1,000—500—he muttered a curse. 'I'll be into the damn carpet in a minute,' was his unspoken thought. He went into a shallow glide, peering below anxiously, praying that his altimeter was functioning properly and that he would not crash into a church tower or a tree. Something dark loomed below and for a minute he could not make out what it was. 'My God! It's the sea,' he ejaculated, and thrusting the throttle wide open he began climbing swiftly.

For a moment the discovery left him stunned. 'Where the devil have I got to?' he said to himself, half in anger and half in fright; 'I ought to have crossed the coast half an hour ago; this damn compass is all wrong, I expect.' He climbed above the mist and for another fifteen minutes flew south and then dropped down again. Something dark reared up in front of him and he zoomed swiftly to avoid hitting a tree, but an exclamation of relief escaped his lips as he saw that he was, at least, over terra firma. 'What a hell of a day!' he muttered again, and once more climbed up above the swirling fog, realizing that if conditions did not improve he would be lucky to get down without damaging the machine and possibly himself. In all directions the fog stretched in an unbroken sea of glistening white. 'This is no use,' he mused; 'I'd better find out where I am—it might as well be now as later on.'

He throttled back once more and commenced another slow glide towards the ground. At 500 feet he could just see what appeared to be open fields below.

He S-turned, almost at stalling point, keenly alert for any possible obstruction. When he was satisfied that all was clear he tipped up his wing and sideslipped down; he levelled out, switched off the ignition, and a moment later ran to a standstill not ten yards from a thick hedge. For a few moments he sat contemplating his predicament, and then climbed slowly out of the cockpit. 'I suppose all I can do is to walk until I find a house or somebody who can tell me where I am,' he reflected ruefully, as, pushing up his goggles and loosening his throat-strap, he set off at a steady pace across the field. He was glad of his short, leather coat, for the ground-mist was cold and clammy.

A hedge loomed up in front of him and he faced it blankly. 'Which way now?' he asked of himself. He thrust his hand in his trouser-pocket and pulled out a coin. 'Heads left, tails right,' he muttered. 'Heads, eh, left it is then'; and he once more set off parallel with the hedge. A hundred yards and another hedge appeared dimly in front of him and he swore luridly. 'Let's have a look what's over the other side,' he muttered, as he took a flying leap and landed on top of it. A sunken road, or rather a cart track, lay before him. 'I wish this blasted mist would clear,' he muttered petulantly, as he set off down the road. 'Hullo! Here's signs of life anyway.' On his right was a row of poles which reminded him of the hop fields he had often seen in Kent; a thick layer of greenery was spread over the tops of the wires that connected them. 'Hell, don't tell me I'm back home again,' he said, aghast. 'No, by God; it's camouflage!' He paused in his stride to survey what was the finest and certainly the largest piece of camouflage he had ever seen. Below it the ground fell away suddenly into a steep dip, and across the intervening valley stretched row after row of posts, criss-crossed at the top with wires, and the whole covered with a layer of drab green canvas and imitation grass.

'Whew!' he whistled; 'whatever's under that would take a bit of spotting from the air.' He bent down and peered below the concealing canopy, but could only see what appeared to be a number of grey cisterns and cylinders. 'Beats me,' he muttered, as he continued his walk. 'Well, here's someone coming, anyway, so we'll soon know.' On the left a gate opened into the field he had just left, and he leaned against it carelessly awaiting the arrival of the owners of the approaching footsteps. 'It sounds like troops,' was his unspoken thought as he lit a cigarette and gazed pensively into the grey mist that hung like a blanket over the field. The footsteps of marching men were close now, and he turned casually in their direction.

The sight that met his eyes seemed to freeze his heart into a block of ice. The shock was so great that he did not move, but stood rigid as if he had been transformed into a block of granite. Out of the mist, not ten yards away, straight down the middle of the road, marched a squad of grey-clad steel-helmeted German soldiers, an N.C.O. at their head. Biggles looked at them with a face of stone, praying that they would not hear the tumultous beating of his heart. There was a sharp word of command; as in a dream he saw the N.C.O.'s hand go up in salute, and his return of the salute was purely automatic. Another word of command and the troops had disappeared into the mist.

For a full minute Biggles gazed after them, utterly and completely stunned, and then a thousand thoughts flooded into his brain at once. Nauseating panic seized him, and he ran to and fro in agitated uncertainty. Never before had he experienced anything like the sensation of helplessness that possessed him now. 'Steady, steady, you fool!' he snarled, as he fought to get a grip on himself. 'Think—think!' Sanity returned at last and he listened intently. In the distance someone was hammering metal against metal. 'Clang! clang! clang! boomed the sound dully through the enveloping mist. 'They took me for one of their own pilots—of course they would. Why should they expect a British pilot to be standing gaping at them? Thank God I had my coat on,' were thoughts that rushed through his mind.

A little father down the road a large notice faced him, and he wondered how he had failed to see it before.

ACHTUNG! LEBENSGEFAHR

CHLORGASANSTALT

EINTRITT STRENG

VERBOTEN*

Chlorgasanstalt! Gas! In an instant he understood everything; the camouflage covered a Hun gas manufacturing plant. 'I'll be getting out of this,' he muttered, and vaulting over the gate set off at a run across the field in the direction of the Camel. Another hedge faced him; he struggled through it and found himself in a field of roots. 'This isn't it,' he muttered hoarsely, and realized with horror that he had lost his sense of direction. He clambered back into the field he had just left

* Danger! Public warning:
Gas plant
Entrance strictly forbidden.

and raced down the side of the hedge, pulling up with a cry of despair as the edge of a wood suddenly faced him. He knew he was lost. 'Damn and blast this fog; where the hell am I?' he groaned out viciously. It was suddenly lighter and he glanced upwards; the mist was lifting at last, slowly, but already he could see the silvery disc of the sun. 'The Boche'll see the Camel as soon as I shall,' he pondered, hopelessly, 'and the farther I go now the farther I shall get away from it. If they spot it, I'm sunk. Oh, hell!' Another thought occurred to him—what of his discovery? Quite apart from saving his own skin he was now in possession of information which the Headquarters Staff would willingly give fifty officers to possess—the whereabouts of the German gas supply dump.

'If I do get away I can't tell them where it is,' he mused; 'I don't know where I am to within a hundred miles. Blast that compass!' He started; someone was coming towards him. He dived into the undergrowth and crouched low, scarcely daring to breathe. The newcomer was a Belgian peasant, garbed in the typical garments of a worker on the land; in his hand he carried a hedger's hook. He was a filthy specimen of his class, dirty and unshaven, and Biggles watched him anxiously as he plodded along muttering to himself, glancing from time to time to left and right. 'I wonder if I dare risk speaking—if he would help me?' thought Biggles. But the risk was too great and he dismissed the idea from his mind. The peasant was opposite him now, snivelling and wiping his nose on the back of his hand; he stopped suddenly and listened intently.

'Where are you?'

The words, spoken in English in a quick sibilant hiss from somewhere near at hand, stunned Biggles into a frozen state of immobility for the second time within a quarter of an hour. His heart seemed to stop beating and he felt the blood drain from his face. Who had spoken? Had anybody spoken—or had he imagined it? Were his nerves giving out? He didn't know, but he bit his lip to prevent himself crying out.

'Where are you?'

Again came the words in a low penetrating whisper, but in an educated English voice.

'Here,' said Biggles involuntarily.

The peasant swung round on his heel and hurried towards him. 'Your machine is in the next field,' he said quickly; 'hurry up, you've no time to lose. Fifty yards—Look out—get down!'

Biggles flung himself back into the undergrowth and pressed himself into the bottom of the ditch that skirted the wood. The peasant's hook flashed above him and a tangle of briars covered him. Through them Biggles could just see the Belgian lopping at the hedge unconcernedly, muttering to himself as he did so. Gutteral voices jarred the silence somewhere near at hand and a group of German soldiers, carrying mess tins, loomed into his field of vision. Without so much as a glance at the hedge trimmer they passed on and were swallowed up in the mist.

'Quick now,' said the voice again, 'run for it. There's an archie battery fifty yards down there—you were walking straight into it; I saw you land, and I've been chasing you ever since.'

'What about the gasworks?' said Biggles irrelevantly.

The pseudo-Belgian started violently. 'What gasworks?' he said, in a curiously strained voice.

'The Hun gas dump,' replied Biggles.

'Where is it?'

'Just across there at the corner of the wood, it's well camouflaged.'

'God Almighty! You've stumbled on the thing I've been looking for for three weeks. Get back and report it in case I am taken before I can loose a carrier pigeon. Here comes the sun—turn right down the hedge, fifty yards, then get through the hedge and you will see the machine in front of you.'

'Where am I now?' inquired Biggles.

'Thirty kilos north-west of Courtrai—one mile due east of Berslaade.'

'Aren't you coming, I can take you on the wing?'

'No, I'll stay here and see what damage the bombers do.'

'What's your name?' asked Biggles quickly.

'2742,' replied the other with a queer smile.

'Mine's Bigglesworth—266 Squadron. Look me up sometime—good-bye.'

A swift handshake and Biggles was sprinting down the side of the hedge in the direction indicated by his preserver.

'God! What jobs some people have to do. I wouldn't have that fellow's job for a million a year and a thousand V.C.s,' thought Biggles, as, fifty yards down the hedge, he crawled through a convenient gap. As he sprang erect the mist rolled away as if a giant curtain had been drawn, and the sun poured down in all its autumnal glory. There, ten yards away, stood the Camel, and beside it two German soldiers. They carried mess tins, and were evidently two of the party he had seen a few moments before.

With a bound, almost without pausing to think, Biggles was on them. The Germans swung round in alarm as they heard his swift approach, but Biggles

held all the advantages of surprise attack. The first
went down like a log before he had time to put his
hands up as his jaw stopped a mighty swing from
Biggles's right; the iron mess-tin rolled to one side as
he fell. Biggles snatched it up by the strap and swung
it with all his force straight at the head of the other
German. It caught the man fairly and squarely on the
temple and he dropped with a grunt like a pole-axed
bullock. The whole thing was over almost before
Biggles had realized the danger. With feverish speed
he sprang to the cockpit of the Camel, switched on,
turned the petrol on, and opened the throttle a fraction.
Dashing back to the front of the machine he paused to
feel the cylinders of the Bentley engine. They were not
yet cold. He seized the propeller and whirled it with
all his strength, almost falling backwards as it started
with a roar. He tore madly round the wing and literally
fell into the cockpit; once there, all his old confidence
returned in a flash and he looked eagerly around. Behind
him the field stretched open for a take-off; in the far
corner some men were running, pointing at him as they
ran. He blipped the engine with the rudder hard over
almost swinging the Camel round on its own axis, and
for the first time since he realized he was in enemy
country, he breathed freely. He pushed the throttle
open and tore across the field like a blunt-nosed
bullet; a moment later he was in the air heading for the
line, with the landscape lying clear and plain below him.

A stab of orange flame and a cloud of black smoke
blossomed out in front of him, another, and another,
and Biggles twisted like a snipe to throw the archie
gunners off their mark. Strings of flaming onions* shot

* Slang: a type of incendiary anti-aircraft shell only used by Germans.

past him and the sky was torn with fire and hurtling metal.

'Hell's bells! they're taking damn good care no one comes prowling about here for long,' he observed, as he kicked out first one foot and then the other to maintain his erratic course in order to confuse the batteries below. He was glad when the storm died down behind him. He surveyed the sky ahead intently. 'They saw me take off and they'll phone every damn aerodrome between here and the line to be on the look-out for me,' he swore to himself. With his nose slightly down and engine at full throttle he sped onwards.

An aerodrome appeared ahead; he could see little ant-like figures running around the black-crossed machines which stood on the tarmac. Something struck the Camel with a vibrating sprang—g—g, and he knew the machine-gunners were busy. He put his nose down in a fury and swept across the hangars with his guns spurting a double stream of tracer, and laughed as he saw the figures below sprinting for cover. He zoomed up and roared on without waiting to see what damage he had done.

A Fokker triplane, looking like a Venetian blind, flashed down on his flank and the sight sent him fighting mad. The Camel made the lightning right-hand turn for which it was famous and the twin Vickers guns on the cowling poured a stream of bullets through the Fokker's centre section. The Boche machine lurched drunkenly and plunged down out of sight below, and Biggles continued his way without another glance. Far away to his left he could see a formation of straight-winged machines heading towards him, and he swept still lower, literally hopping the trees and hedges that stood in his path. The pock-marked desolation of the trenches appeared below and Biggles thrilled at the sight; he shot across them at fifty feet, wondering vaguely where all the bullets that were being fired at him were going.

He was over his own side of the lines now, and he sagged lower in the cockpit with relief as he passed the balloon line. Ten minutes later he landed at Maranique. Major Mullen was standing on the tarmac and came to meet him as he taxied in.

'You've got back then, Biggles—had a good leave?'

'Fine, sir, thanks,' responded Biggles.

'It's been pretty thick here. What time did you leave this morning?'

'Oh, about sixish.'

'Then you must have called somewhere on the way—I hope they gave you a good time?'

'They did that,' grinned Biggles as he climbed out of the cockpit.

Major Mullen eyed his mud-plastered boots and coat with astonishment. 'Good God!' he cried, 'where the devil have you been?'

'On leave, sir,' smiled Biggles innocently, 'but I've got an urgent message for H.Q.'

In a few words he described his adventures of the morning, and ten minutes later his written report was on its way by hand to Headquarters. One thing only he omitted—his finding of the gas plant. He reported its position, but the credit for that discovery he left to '2742.' 'That's the least I can do for him,' decided Biggles.

Chapter 16
Affaire De Cœur*

Biggles hummed cheerfully as he cruised along in the new Camel which he had just fetched from the Aircraft Park. 'Another five minutes and I shall be home,' he thought, but fate willed otherwise. The engine coughed, coughed again, and with a final splutter, expired, leaving him with a 'dead' prop. He swore softly, pushed the joystick forward, and looked quickly around for the most suitable field for the now inevitable forced landing.

To the right lay the forest of Clarmes. 'Nothing doing that way,' he muttered, and looked down between his left wings. Ah! there it was. Almost on the edge of the forest was a large pasture, free from obstruction. The pilot, with a confidence born of long experience, sideslipped towards it, levelled out over the hedge and made a perfect three-point landing.

He sat in the cockpit for a minute or two contemplating his position, then he yawned, pushed up his goggles and prepared to take stock of his immediate surroundings. He raised his eyebrows appreciatively as he noted the sylvan beauty of the scene around him. Above, the sun shone from a cloudless blue sky. Straight before him a low lichen-covered stone wall enclosed an orchard through which he could just perceive a dull red pantiled roof. To the right lay the forest, cool and

* French: an affair of the heart.

inviting. To the left a stream meandered smoothly between a double row of willows.

'Who said there was a war on?' he murmured, lighting a cigarette, and climbing up on to the 'hump' of his Camel, the better to survey the enchanting scene. 'Well, well, let's see if anyone is at home.' He sprang lightly to the ground, threw his leather coat across the fuselage and strolled towards the house. An old iron gate opened into the orchard; entering, he paused for a moment, uncertain of the path.

'Are you looking for me, monsieur?' said a voice, which sounded to Biggles as musical as ice tinkling in a cocktail glass.

Turning, he beheld a vision of blonde loveliness wrapped up in blue silk, smiling at him. For a moment he stared as if he had been raised in a monastery and had never seen a woman before. He closed his eyes, shook his head, and opened them again—the vision was still there, dimpling.

'You were looking for me, perhaps?' said the girl again.

Biggles saluted like a man sleep-walking.

'Mademoiselle,' he said earnestly, 'I've been looking for you all my life. I didn't think I'd ever find you.'

'Then why did you land here?' asked the girl.

'I landed here because my mag. shorted,' explained Biggles.

'What would have happened if you had not landed when your bag shorted?' inquired the vision, curiously.

'Not bag—mag. Short for magneto, you know,' replied Biggles grinning. 'Do you know, I've never even thought of doing anything but land when a mag. shorts; if I didn't, I expect that I should fall from a great altitude and collide with something substantial.'

177

'What are you going to do now?'

'I don't know—it takes thinking about. It may be necessary for me to stay here for some time. Anyway, the War will still be on when I get back. But, pardon me, mademoiselle, if I appear impertinent; are you English? I ask because you speak English so well.'

'Not quite, monsieur. My mother was English and I have been to school in England,' replied the girl.

'Thank you, Miss—er—'

'Marie Janis is my name.'

'A charming name, more charming even than this spot of heaven,' said Biggles warmly. 'Have you a telephone, Miss Janis? You see, although the matter is not urgent, if I do not ring up my Squadron to say where I am, someone may fly around to look for me,' he explained.

The thought of Mahoney spotting his Camel from the air and landing, did not, in the circumstances, fill him with the enthusiasm one might normally expect.

'Come and use the telephone, m'sieur le Capitaine,' said the girl, leading the way. 'May I offer you *un petit verre**?'

'May you?' responded Biggles, warmly. 'I should say you may!'

Five hours later Biggles again took his place in the cockpit of the Camel which a party of ack-emmas had now repaired. He took off and swung low over the orchard, waving gaily to a slim blue-clad figure that looked upwards and waved back.

Rosy clouds drifted across the horizon as he made the short flight back to the aerodrome.

'That girl's what I've been reading about,' he told

*French: a little glass of something.

178

himself. 'She's the "Spirit of the Air," and she's going to like me an awful lot if I know anything about it. Anyway, I'd be the sort of skunk who'd give rat poison to orphans if I didn't go back and thank her for her hospitality.

Biggles, a week later, seated on an old stone bench in the orchard, sighed contentedly. The distant flickering beam of a searchlight on the war-stricken sky meant nothing to him; the rumble of guns along the line seemed very far away. His arm rested along the back of the seat; a little head, shining whitely in the moonlight, nestled lightly on his sleeve. In the short time that had elapsed since his forced landing, he had made considerable progress.

'Tell me, Marie,' he said, 'do you ever hear from your father?'

'No, m'sieur,' replied the girl sadly. 'I told you he was on a visit to the north when war was declared. In the wild panic of the Boche advance he was left behind in what is now the occupied territory. Communication with that part of France is forbidden, but I have had two letters from him which were sent by way of England by friends. I have not even been able to tell him that maman is—dead!'

Tears shone for a moment in her eyes, and Biggles stirred uncomfortably.

'It is a hell of a war,' he said compassionately.

'If only I could get a letter to him to say that maman—*est mort**, and that I am looking after things until he returns, I should be happy. Poor Papa!'

* French: is dead.

'I suppose you don't even know where he is?' said Biggles sympathetically.

'But yes,' answered the girl quickly, 'I know where he is. He is still at our friend's château, where he was staying when the Boche came.'

'Where's that?' asked Biggles in surprise.

'At Vinard, near Lille; le Château Boreau,' she replied, 'but he might as well be in Berlin,' she concluded sadly, shrugging her shoulders.

'Good Lord!' ejaculated Biggles suddenly.

'Why did you say that, monsieur?'

'Nothing—only an idea struck me, that's all,' said Biggles.

'Tell me.'

'No. I'm crazy. Better forget it.'

'Tell me—please.'

Biggles wavered. 'All right,' he said, 'say "please Biggles," and I'll tell you.'

'Please, Beegles.'

Biggles smiled at the pronunciation. 'Well, if you must know,' he said, 'it struck me that I might act as a messenger for you.'

'Beegles! How?'

'I had some crazy notion that I might be able to drop a letter from my machine,' explained Biggles.

'Mon dieu*!' The girl sprang to her feet in excitement, but Biggles held her arm and pulled her towards him. For a moment she resisted, and then slipped into his arms.

'Beegles—please.'

'Marie,' whispered Biggles, as their lips met. Then, his heart beating faster than archie or enemy aircraft

* French: My God!

180

had ever caused it to beat, he suddenly pushed her aside, rose to his feet and looked at the luminous dial of his watch. 'Time I was getting back to quarters,' he said unsteadily.

'But, Beegles, it is not yet so late.'

Biggles sat down, passed his hand over his face and then laughed. 'My own mag. was nearly shorting then,' he said.

They both laughed, and the spell was broken.

'Tell me, Beegles, is it possible to drop such a letter to papa?' said the girl presently.

'I don't know,' said Biggles, a trifle anxiously. 'I don't know what orders are about that sort of thing, and that's a fact. There wouldn't be any harm in it, and they wouldn't know about it, anyway. You give me the letter and I'll see what I can do.'

'Beegles—you—'

'Well?'

'Never mind. Come to the house and we will write the letter together.'

Hand in hand they walked slowly towards the house. The girl took a writing pad from a desk and began to write; the door opened noiselessly and Antoine, Marie's elderly man-servant appeared.

'Did you ring, mademoiselle?' he asked.

'Merci, Antoine.'

'Do you know,' said Biggles, after the man had withdrawn, 'I don't like the look of that bloke. I never saw a nastier-looking piece of work in my life.'

'But what should I do without Antoine and Lucille, his wife. They are the only two that stayed with me all the time. Antoine is a dear, he only thinks of me,' said the girl reproachfully.

'I see,' said Biggles. 'Well, go ahead with the letter.'

181

The girl wrote rapidly.

'Look,' she smiled when it was finished. 'Read it and tell me if you do not think it is a lovely letter to a long-lost father.'

Biggles read the first few lines and skipped the rest, blushing. 'I don't want to read your letter, kid,' he said.

Marie sealed the letter, addressed it, and tied it firmly to a small paper weight. 'Now,' she said, 'what can we use for a banner?'

'You mean a streamer,' laughed Biggles.

'Yes, a streamer. Why! Here is the very thing.' She took a black and white silk scarf from the back of a chair and tied the paper-weight to it. 'There you are, *mon aviateur**,' she laughed. 'Take care, do not hit papa on the head or he will wish I had not written.'

Biggles slipped the packet into the pocket of his British 'warm'** and took her in his arms impatiently.

Arriving at the aerodrome he went to his quarters and flung the coat on the bed, and then made his way across to the mess for a drink. As the door of his quarters closed behind him, two men—an officer in uniform and a civilian—entered the room. Without a moment's hesitation the civilian picked up the coat and removed the letter from the pocket.

'You know what to do,' he said grimly.

'How long will you be?'

'An hour. Not more. Keep him until 11.30, to be on the safe side,' said the civilian.

'I will,' replied the officer, and followed Biggles into the mess.

---

* French: my pilot.
** Slang: Thick padded jacket.

Biggles, humming gaily, headed for home. His trip had proved uneventful and the dropping of Marie's letter ridiculously simple. He had found the château easily, and swooping low had seen the black and white scarf flutter on to the lawn. Safely back across the line he was now congratulating himself upon the success of his mission. 287, the neighbouring S.E.5 Squadron, lay below, and it occurred to him to land and pass the time of day with them.

Conscious that many eyes would be watching him, he side-slipped in and flattened out for his most artistic landing. There was a sudden crash, the Camel swung violently and tipped up on to its nose. Swearing savagely he climbed out and surveyed the damage.

'Why the devil don't you fellows put a flag or something on this sunken road?' he said bitterly to Wilkinson and other pilots who had hurried to the scene; and pointing to the cause of his misadventure, 'Look at that mess.'

'Well, most people know about that road,' said Wilkinson. 'If I'd have known you were coming I'd have had it filled in altogether. Never mind; it's only a tyre and the prop. gone. Our fellows will have it right by to-morrow. Come and have a drink; I'll find you transport to take you home. The C.O.'s on leave, so you can use his car.'

'Righto, but I'm not staying to dinner,' said Biggles emphatically. 'I'm on duty to-night,' he added, thinking of a moonlit orchard and an old stone seat.

It was nearly eight o'clock when he left the aerodrome, seated at the wheel of the borrowed car. He had rung up Major Mullen and told him that he would be late, and now, thrilling with anticipation, he headed for the home of the girl who was making life worth living and the war worth fighting for.

The night was dark, for low clouds were drifting across the face of the moon; a row of distant archie-bursts made him look up, frowning. A bomb raid, inter-rupting the story of his successful trip, was the last thing he wanted. His frown deepened as the enemy aircraft and the accompanying archie drew nearer. 'They're coming right over the house, blast 'em,' he said, and switching off his lights raced for the orchard. 'God! they're low,' he muttered, as he tore down the road, the roar of the engines of the heavy bombers in his ears. 'They're following this road, too.' He wondered where they were making for, trying to recall any possible objective on their line of flight. That he himself might be in danger did not even occur to him. He was less than five miles from the house now, and taking desperate chances to race the machines. 'The poor kid'll be scared stiff if they pass over her as low as this.'

With every nerve taut he tore down the road. He caught his breath suddenly. What was that! A whistling screech filled his ears and an icy hand clutched his heart. Too well he knew the sound. Boom! Boom! Boom! Three vivid flashes of orange fire leapt towards the sky. Boom! Boom! Boom!—and then three more.

'My God! what are they fanning, the fools? There is only the forest there,' thought Biggles, as, numb with shock, he raced round the last bend. Six more thunder-ing detonations, seemingly a hundred yards ahead, nearly split his eardrums, but still he did not pause. He tried to think, but could not; he had lost all sense of time and reason. He seemed to have been driving for ever, and he cursed as he drove. Searchlights probed the sky on all sides and subconsciously he noticed that the noise of the engines was fading into the distance.

'They've gone,' he said, trying hard to think clearly. 'God! If they've hit the house!' He jammed on his brakes with a grinding screech as two men sprang out in front of the car as he turned in the gates, but he was not looking at them. One glance showed him that the house was a blazing pile of ruins. He sprang out of the car and darted towards the conflagration, but a hand closed on his arm like a vice. Biggles, white-faced, turned and struck out viciously. 'My girl's in there, blast you,' he muttered.

A sharp military voice penetrated his stunned brain. 'Stand fast, Captain Bigglesworth,' it said.

'Let me go, damn you,' snarled Biggles, struggling like a madman.

'One more word from you, Captain Bigglesworth, and I'll put you under close arrest,' said the voice harshly.

'You'll what?' Biggles turned, his brain fighting for consciousness. 'You'll what?' he cried again incredulously. He saw the firelight gleam on the fixed bayonets of a squad of Tommies; Colonel Raymond of Wing Headquarters and another man stood near them. Biggles passed his hand over his eyes, swaying.

'I'm dreaming,' he said, 'that's it, dreaming. God! what a hell of a nightmare. I wish I could wake up.'

'Take a drink, Bigglesworth, and pull yourself together,' said Colonel Raymond passing him a flask. Biggles emptied the flask and handed it back.

'I'm going now,' said the Colonel, 'I'll see you in the morning. This officer will tell you all you need to know,' he concluded, indicating a dark-clad civilian standing near. 'Good-night, Bigglesworth.'

'Good-night, sir.'

'Tell me,' said Biggles, with an effort, 'is she—in there?'

The man nodded.

'Then, that's all I need to know,' said Biggles, slowly turning away.

'I'm sorry, but there are other things you will have to know,' returned the man.

'Who are you?' said Biggles curiously.

'Major Charles, of the British Intelligence Service.'

'Intelligence!' repeated Biggles, the first ray of light bursting upon him.

'Come here a moment.' Major Charles switched on the lights of his car. 'Yesterday, a lady asked you to deliver a message for her, did she not?' he asked.

'Why—yes.'

'Did you see it?'

'Yes!'

'Was this it?' said Major Charles, handing him a letter.

Biggles read the first few lines, dazed. 'Yes,' he said, 'that was it.'

'Turn it over.'

Unconsciously Biggles obeyed. He started as his eyes fell on a tangle of fine lines that showed up clearly. In the centre was a circle.

'Do you recognize that?'

'Yes.'

'What is it?'

'It is a map of 266 Squadron aerodrome,' replied Biggles, like a child reciting a catechism.

'You see the circle?'

'Yes.'

'The Officers' mess. Perhaps you understand now.

The letter you were asked to carry had been previously prepared with a solution of invisible ink and contained such information that, had you delivered it, your entire squadron would have been wiped out to-night, and you as well. The girl sent you to your death, Captain Bigglesworth.'

'I'll not believe it,' said Biggles distinctly. 'But I did deliver the letter, anyway,' he cried suddenly.

'Not this one,' said Major Charles smiling queerly. 'You delivered the one we substituted.'

'Substituted!'

'We have watched this lady for a long time. You have been under surveillance since the day you force-landed, although your record put you above suspicion.'

'And on the substituted plan you marked her home to be bombed instead of the aerodrome?' sneered Biggles. 'Why?'

Major Charles shrugged his shoulders. 'The lady was well connected. There may have been unexpected difficulties connected with an arrest, yet her activities had to be checked. She had powerful friends in high places. Well, I must be going; no doubt you will hear from Wing in the morning.'

Biggles walked a little way up the garden path. The old stone seat glowed dully crimson. 'Bah!' he muttered, turning, 'what a fool I am. What a hell of a war this is.'

He drove slowly back to the aerodrome. On his table lay a letter. Ripping it open eagerly he read:—

'CHÈR*,

'I have something important to ask you—some-

* French: Dear.

187

thing you must do for me. To-night at seven o'clock
I will come for you. It is important. Meet me in the
road by the aerodrome. I will be very kind to you,
my Biggles.

MARIE.'

Biggles, with trembling hands, sat on the bed and
reread the letter, trying to reason out its purport. 'She
timed the raid for eight,' he said to himself, 'when all
officers would be dining in mess. She knew I should be
there and wrote this to bring me out. She knew I'd
never leave her waiting on the road—that was the way
of it. She must have cared, or she wouldn't have done
that. When I didn't come she went back home. She
didn't even know I hadn't seen her letter—how could
she? Now she's dead. If I hadn't landed at 287 I should
be with her now. Well, she'll never know.' He rose
wearily. Voices were singing in the distance, and he
smiled bitterly as he heard the well-remembered
words:—

> Who minds to the dust returning,
>   Who shrinks from the sable shore,
> Where the high and haughty yearning
>   Of the soul shall be no more?
>
> So stand by your glasses steady,
>   This world is a world of lies;
> A cup to the dead already,
>   Hurrah! for the next man who dies.

A knock at the door aroused him from his reverie.
An orderly of the guard entered.

'A lady left this for you,' he said, holding out a letter.

'A lady?—when?' said Biggles, holding himself in hand with a mighty effort.

'About ten minutes ago, sir. Just before you came in. She came about eight and said she must see you, sir, but I told her you weren't here.'

'Where is she now?'

'She's gone, sir, she was in a car. She told me to bring the letter straight to you when you returned, sir.'

'All right—you may go.'

Biggles took the letter, fighting back a wild desire to shout, opened it, and read:

'Good-bye, my Biggles.

'You know now. What can I say? Only this. Our destinies are not always in our own hands—always try and remember that, my Biggles. That is all I may say. I came to-night to take you away or die with you, but you were not here. And remember that one thing in this world of war and lies is true: my love for you. It may help you, as it helps me. Take care of yourself. Always I shall pray for you. If anything happens to you I shall know, but if to me, you will never know. My last thought will be of you. We shall meet again, if not in this world then in the next, so I will not say good-bye.

'Au revoir,

'MARIE.'

'And they think she's dead,' said Biggles softly. 'She risked her life to tell me this.' He kissed the letter tenderly, then held it to the candle and watched it burn away.

He was crumbling the ashes between his fingers

when the door opened, and Mahoney entered. 'Hullo! laddie, what's wrong; had a fire?' he inquired.

'Yes,' replied Biggles slowly, 'foolish of me; got my fingers burnt a bit, too.'

Chapter 17
The Last Show

In the days that followed his tragic *affaire*, Biggles flew
with an abandon and with such an utter disregard
of consequences, that Major Mullen knew that if he
persisted it could only be a matter of time before he
failed to return. The C.O. had not mentioned the affair
of the girl to him, but Biggles knew that he must be
aware of the main facts of the case, or he would certainly have asked him why he had been called to Headquarters.

However much the Major knew he said nothing, but
he watched his Flight-Commander's behaviour with
deep-rooted anxiety. He called McLaren and Mahoney
into his office to discuss the matter with them.

Mahoney nodded sympathetically as he listened to
the C.O.'s plaint. 'Biggles is finished unless he takes a
rest,' he said. 'He's drinking whisky for his breakfast,
and you know what that means—he's going fast. He
drank half a bottle of whisky yesterday morning before
daylight, and he walked up to the sheds as sober as I
was. A fellow doesn't get drunk when he's in the state
Biggles is in. It's no use talking to him—you know that
as well as I do. He's got to the stage when he takes
advice as a personal affront against his flying. It's a
pity, but most of us go that way at the end I suppose.
Newland, of 287, told me confidentially the other day
that a blue pigeon follows him in the air wherever he
goes, and he meant it.'

'Well, I shall have to send him home, whether he likes it or not,' went on the Major, 'but it will break his heart if I don't find a good excuse. Now look, you fellows. I've got to send somebody home to form a new Squadron—of Snipes*, I believe—and bring it over. You are both senior to Bigglesworth; you are both due for promotion. I shall be going to Wing in a week or two I hear, so one of you will have to take over 266. Do you mind if I send Bigglesworth home for the new Squadron?' added the C.O., looking at the two Captains apologetically.

'Not me, sir,' said Mahoney instantly.

'Nor I, sir,' echoed McLaren.

'Thank you. That's what I wanted to know,' said the Major. 'I'll send him home, then. Where is he now?'

'He's in the air,' replied Mahoney, 'he's never on the ground. God knows where he goes, it must be miles over; I never see him on patrol.'

The C.O. nodded. 'Well, he can't get away with that much longer. They're bound to get him. By the way, there's a big show tomorrow—it will be in orders tonight. You'd better have a good look round your machines.'

Biggles, cruising at 18,000 feet, turned in the direction of Lille without being really conscious of the fact. He surveyed the surrounding air coldly and dispassionately for signs of enemy aircraft, but except for a formation of Bristol Fighters homeward bound, far below, the sky was empty. His thoughts wandered back to the girl who had come into his life. Where was she now? Where

* Sopwith Snipe – a development of the Sopwith Camel, with slightly better performance.

192

had she gone on that tragic night of disillusionment? Had she been caught? That was the thought that made the day a torture and night a hell. He visualized her in the cold-grey of dawn with a bandage over her eyes facing a firing party in some gloomy French prison.

A volley of shots rang out, something jerked the rudder-bar from his feet and brought him back to the realities of life with a start.

He half-rolled and looked around; a Hannoverian was rapidly receding into the distance. He frowned at it in surprise and consternation. 'Good Lord! I must have nearly flown into it without seeing it, and the observer had a crack at me as he went by,' he mused. 'If it had been a D.VII'—he shrugged his shoulders. What did it matter—what did anything matter?

He looked downwards to pick up his bearings; the landscape was familiar, for he had seen it a dozen times during the past week. To the left lay Lille, the worst hot-bed of archie in the whole of France. On his right a narrow, winding road led to the village of Vinard and the Château Boreau—his only link with Marie. She might even be there now—the thought occurred to him for the first time. How could she have reached it? Spies went to and fro across the line, he reflected, nobody knew how, except the chosen few whose hazardous business it was. He looked around the sky, but could see nothing; he put the stick forward and commenced to spiral down in wide circles.

At 5,000 feet he hesitated. Dare he risk losing more height? He looped, half-rolled, came out and looped again, half-rolling off the top of it. Then he spun. He came out at 2,000 feet and studied the château intently. No one was in sight—yes—his eye caught a movement at the end of the garden and he glided lower. He knew that he was taking a foolish risk, but his curiosity overcame his caution.

Someone was waving—what? He put his nose down in a swift dive and then zoomed upwards exultantly, his heart beating tumultuously. Had his eyes betrayed him or had he seen a blue-clad figure waving a blue and white scarf. He looked back; the blue and white scarf was spread on the lawn. He turned the Camel in the direction of the lines and raced for home, his mind in a whirl. 'I'm mad,' he grated between his clenched teeth. She must be a spy or she wouldn't be there. The thought seemed to chill him, and only then did he realize that he still hoped the authorities were mistaken in their belief that she was engaged in espionage.

Doubts began to assail him. Had he really seen her— or had it been a trick of the imagination? It might have been someone else; he was too far away to recognize features. 'She's a spy, anyway. I must be stark, staring mad,' he told himself, as he dodged and twisted away from a close salvo of archie.

Half-way home he had the good fortune to fall in with a formation of S.E.5's to which he attached himself. Safely over the lines he waved them farewell and was soon back at Maranique. He made his way to the mess and thrust himself into a group of officers clustered around the notice board.

'What's on, chaps?' he asked.

'Big show tomorrow, Biggles,' replied Mahoney.

'What is it?'

'Escort—a double dose. Eighteen "Nines" are bombing aerodrome 27 in the morning and the same lot are doing an objective near Lille in the afternoon. We and 287 are escorting. 287 are up in the gallery, and we're

194

sticking with the formation. Rendezvous over Mossy-face at 10,000 feet at ten ack-emma.'

'Good God! have they discovered the German Head-quarters Staff or something?'

'Shouldn't be surprised. Must be something important to do the two shows. The aerodrome 27 show was on first—and the second show came through later. They must be going to try and blot something off the map; the idea's all right if the bombers could only hit the thing.'

Biggles nodded moodily, for the show left him unmoved. Escort was a boring business, particularly in his present state of mind. Later in the evening another notice was put on the board which was greeted with loud cheers. Biggles forced his way to the front rank of the group and read:

Promotions
Act. Cpt. J. Bigglesworth, M.C., to Major W.E.F.*
10.11.18. (*Authority*) P.243/117/18.
Postings
Major J. Bigglesworth, from 266 Squadron to Command 319 Squadron. H.E., W.E.F.** 11.11.18. P.243/118/18.

Biggles looked at the notice, unbelievingly. He turned to Major Mullen, who had just entered.

'So I'm going home, sir,' he said in a strained voice.

'Yes, Bigglesworth. Wing wants you to fetch 319 out. I believe you're getting Snipes—you'll be able to make rings round Camels.'

'Camels are good enough for me,' protested Biggles. 'That's the trouble with this damn war; people are

* With Effect From.
** Home Establishment (i.e. England) With Effect From.

never satisfied. Let us stick to Camels and S.E.'s and the Boche have their D. Sevens—damn all this chopping and changing about. I've heard a rumour about a new kite called a Salamander* that carries a sheet of armour plate. Why? I'll tell you. Some brass-hat's got hit in the pants and that's the result. What with sheet iron, oxygen to blow your guts out, and electrically heated clothing to set fire to your kidneys, this war is going to bits.'

'You'll talk differently when you get your Snipes,' laughed the Major.

'Orders say I'm to move off tomorrow.'

'Yes, that's right.'

'Good. You can give my love to the Huns at aerodrome 27 and—what's the name of the other target they're going to fan down?'

'Oh, it's a new one to me,' replied the Major. 'Place near Lille, Château Boreau or something like that—cheerio—see you later.'

It was as well that he did not pause to take a second glance at his Flight-Commander's face, or he might have asked awkward questions. For a full minute Biggles remained rooted to the spot with the words ringing in his ears. 'Château Boreau, eh?' he said, under his breath. 'So they know about that. My God! how the devil did those nosey-parkers on Intelligence find that out,' he muttered bitterly.

Mahoney slapped him on the back. 'Have a drink, Biggles?' he cried.

Biggles swung round with a curse. 'No, I didn't mean that, old lad,' he said quickly. 'I was a bit upset at

* Sopwith Salamander. British single seat biplane, designed for use against infantry, fitted with two machine guns and protective armour to the cockpit.

leaving the Squadron. Sorry—what are you having, everybody?' he called aloud. 'Drinks are on me tonight.'

Dinner was a boistrous affair; the usual farewell speeches were made and everybody was noisily happy. Biggles, pale-faced, with his eyes gleaming unnaturally, held the board.

'So tomorrow I am doing my last show,' he concluded.

The C.O. looked up quickly. 'But I thought you were going in the morning,' he exclaimed in surprise.

'In the afternoon, if you don't mind, sir,' answered Biggles, 'I must do one more show with 266.'

Major Mullen nodded. 'All right,' he said, 'but don't take any chances,' he added. 'I ought to pack you off in the morning, really.'

Biggles spent a troubled and restless night. Why he had asked to be allowed to fly with the morning show he hardly knew, unless it was to delay departure as long as possible. He racked his brain to find an excuse to postpone it until the evening in order to learn the result of the bombing of the Château. If he was unable to do that, he had decided to ask Mac or Mahoney to try to send him copies of the photographs of the bomb bursts.

Thinking things over, he realized that his first fears that the Château was to be bombed because Intelligence had learned that Marie had made her way there, were unfounded. It was far more likely that they had known for some time that the building housed certain members of the German Headquarters or Intelligence Staff, and the recent trouble had simply served to expedite their decision to bomb it.

What could he do about it? Nothing, he decided despairingly, absolutely nothing. It crossed his mind that he might drop a message of warning, but he dismissed the thought at once, because such an act would definitely make him a traitor to his own side. The thought of returning to England and leaving the girl to her fate without lifting a finger to save her nearly drove him to distraction. After all, the girl had tried to save him when the position had been reversed!

He was glad when his batman brought him his early morning tea and he arose, weary and hollow eyed. Ten o'clock found him in the air heading for the line and the Boche aerodrome at Lille. Behind him were Cowley and Algernon Montgomery. On his left were the bombers, the sun flashing on their varnished wings, the observers leaning carelessly on their Scarff rings. Beyond was Mahoney and A Flight. Somewhere in the rear was McLaren and B Flight, while two thousand feet above he could see the S.E.5's. 'What a sight,' thought Biggles, as his eyes swept over the thirty-six machines; 'it will take a Hun with some nerve to tackle this lot.'

The observer in the nearest 'Nine' waved to him, crossed his fingers and pointed; Biggles following the direction indicated, saw a half-a-dozen Fokker Triplanes flying parallel with them. Presently they turned away and disappeared into the distance. The observer waved and laughed and held out his hands with the thumbs turned up.

'Yes,' agreed Biggles mentally, 'they spotted the S.E.'s up top. They've thought better of it, and I don't wonder.' He was sorry that the Huns had departed, for he was aching for action. For three-quarters of an hour they flew steadily into enemy sky, and then the leader of the bombers conspicuous by his streamers, began to turn. 'He's coming round into the wind,' thought Biggles; 'we must be over the objective.'

He looked down and beheld the aerodrome. He looked up again just in time to see the leader fire a green Very light; eighteen 112-lb. bombs swung off their racks into space.

A moment later a second lot of eighteen bombs followed the first. Keeping a watchful eye on his position in the formation Biggles snatched quick glances at the earth below. What a time it seemed to take the bombs to reach the ground. 'Damn it, they can't all be duds,' he muttered. 'Ah! there they go.' A group of smoke-bursts appeared on the aerodrome, and a moment later, another group.

The second lot were better than the first. One bomb had fallen directly on to a hangar, one had burst among the machines on the tarmac, and another had struck some buildings just behind. The rest of the bombs had scattered themselves over the aerodrome. 'There will have to be a lot of spade work there before anybody will try any night-landings,' grinned Biggles, as he visualized the havoc the bombs had caused to the surface of the aerodrome.

The faint crackle of guns reached his ears above the noise of the engines; he looked quickly over his shoulder and caught his breath as his eyes fell on a mixed swarm of Fokker D.VII's and triplanes coming down almost vertically on the rearmost 'Nines.' The gunners in the back seats were crouching low behind their Lewis guns. For a brief moment, as the enemy came within range, the air was full of sparkling lines of tracer, and then the Fokkers disappeared through and below the bombers.

He saw McLaren's machine wallow for a moment like a rolling porpoise, and then, with the rest of his

Flight, plunge down in the wake of the enemy machines.

'God! There must be thirty of them, and they mean business, coming in like that,' thought Biggles, as he rocked his wings and roared down into the whirling medley below. A red-painted machine crossed his sights and he pressed his triggers, but had to jerk round in a steep bank to avoid colliding with the first of the S.E.'s which were coming down from above. He glanced around swiftly. The air about him was full of machines, diving, zooming and circling; the bombers had held on their course and were already a mile away.

He flung his Camel on the tail of a blue-and-white Fokker, and the same instant there was a splintering jar as something crashed through his instrument board. A burning pain paralysed his leg, and he twisted desperately to try to see his opponent. Huns were all around him shooting his machine to pieces. He pulled the joystick back into his stomach and zoomed wildly. A Fokker flashed into his sights; he saw his tracer pour straight through it; the pilot slumped forward in his seat and the nose of the machine went down in an engine stall as the withering blast of lead struck it.

Something lashed the Camel like a cat-o'-nine-tails; he felt the machine quiver, and the next moment he was spinning, fighting furiously to get the machine on an even keel. A feeling of nauseating helplessness swept over him as he realized the Camel was not answering to the controls.

Something strange seemed to be whirling on the end of his wing-tip, and he saw it was an aileron*, hanging by a single wire. He kicked the opposite rudder and

* Usually a part of the trailing edge of a wing, made to turn the aircraft to left or right by means of a control column.

200

the nose of the Camel came up. 'God!—If I can only keep her there,' was the thought that flashed through his brain; but another burst of fire from an unseen foe tore through his centre section and he instinctively kicked out his right foot. The Camel spun again at once. He was near the ground now and he fought to get the nose of the machine up again, but something seemed to have gone wrong with his leg. He could not move it.

Biggles knew his time had come. He knew he was going down under a hail of lead in just the same way as he had seen dozens of machines going down, as he himself had sent them down. He knew he was going to crash, but the knowledge left him unmoved. A thousand thoughts crowded into his mind in a second of time that seemed like minutes; in that brief moment he thought of a dozen things he might do as the machine struck.

The nose of the Camel half came up—slowly—and the machine stopped spinning.

The Camel was side-slipping steeply to the right now, nose down, on the very verge of another spin that would be the last. The joystick was back in his left thigh and he unfastened his belt and twisted in his seat to get his right foot on the left side of the rudder, but it had no effect. A row of poplars appeared to leap upwards to meet him; he switched off the ignition with a lightning sweep of his hand, lifted the knee of his unwounded leg to his chin, folded his arms across his face and awaited the impact.

There was a splintering, rending crash, like a great tree in a forest falling on to the undergrowth. With the horror of fire upon him he clawed his way frantically out of the tangled wreck and half-rolled and half-crawled away from it. He seemed to be moving in a ghastly nightmare from which he could not awake. He became vaguely aware of the heat of a conflagration near him; it was the Camel, blazing furiously. Strange-looking soldiers were running towards him and he tore off his blood-stained goggles and stared at them, trying to grasp what had happened and what was happening. 'I'm down,' he muttered to himself in a voice which he hardly recognized as his own. 'I'm down,' he said again, as if the sound of the words would help him to understand.

The German soldiers were standing in a circle around him now, and he looked at them curiously. One of them stepped forward; 'Schweinhund flieger*!' he grunted, and kicked him viciously in the side. Biggles bit his lip at the pain. The man raised his heavy boot again, but there was a sudden authoritative word of command and he stepped back hastily. Biggles looked up to see an officer of about his own age, in a tight-fitting pale-grey uniform, regarding him compassionately. He noted the Pour-le-Merite Order at his throat, and the Iron Cross of the First Class below.

'So you have had bad luck,' he said, in English, with scarcely a trace of accent.

'Yes,' replied Biggles with an effort, forcing a smile and trying to get on to his feet. 'And I am sorry it happened this morning.'

'Why?'

'Because I particularly wanted to see a raid this afternoon,' he answered.

'Yes? But there will be no raid this afternoon,' replied the German smiling.

* German: Pilot swine!

'Why not?'

The German laughed softly. 'An armistice* was signed half an hour ago—but of course, you didn't know.'

---

* Peace, the end of the War. Signed 11 o'clock, 11 November 1918. Remembered today by Poppy Day.